|| राधे-राधे ||

ABOUT THE AUTHOR

The journey started when Naman Mishra, went for his graduation and there he met some really great people who inspired him to write, to focus on the orthodox issues prevailing in the society. Not only that, there were many things that took place in his surroundings which changed his way of thinking and made him more anxious to write as well as share his own personal stories.

Naman is pursuing his Master of Arts in Economics and also, he is working practically on the field pf Economics and contributing to the same by carrying out various research. Naman is ambitious, while focusing on all issues, stigmas and stereotypes that others go through. Naman's journey continues as he uses his writing and research to inspire positive change in the world.

✉ mnaman225@gmail.com
@naman_mishra5
@Naman Mishra

NAMAN MISHRA

Made with ♥ on the Notion Press Platform

www.notionpress.com

DEDICATED TO

Everyone who is courageous enough to love and brave enough to accept the harsh reality of life.

Through the book we intend to take the readers into an immersive rollercoaster journey with no intentions to hurt or harm anyone. All the characters in the book are purely fictional and the author does not endorse any actions made by the same.

PROLOGUE

In the numerous battles of life, there exists a constant battle between the head and the heart. It is a struggle as old as time, a delicate balance between rational thought and emotional longing. Our hearts yearn for connection, love, and the warmth of shared moments, while our minds seek stability, reason, and the comfort of knowing our place in the world. This timeless conflict often shapes the paths we tread, defining the choices we make and the lives we lead.

The story that unfolds within these pages is a testament to that eternal struggle. It is a tale of love and loss, of holding on and letting go. It is about Yajat and Swarnima, a journey of profound introspection and emotional upheaval. As they navigate the highs and lows of their relationship, they grapple with the weight of their decisions and the impact of their actions. This is an invitation to delve into their world, to witness the heart-wrenching moments of separation and the bittersweet realization that love can take many forms. It is a reminder that in the battle between the head and the heart, there are no easy answers, only the hope that through understanding and acceptance, we can find peace.

As you turn the pages, may you find solace in their journey, and perhaps, a reflection of your own battles within. For in the end, we all strive to find that delicate balance, to learn the art of letting go, and to embrace the journey that lies ahead.

CHAPTER I

THE END & BEGINNING

In the bustling city of Delhi, amidst the symphony of honking horns and bustling streets, there resided a young man named Yajat. With his tall, lean frame and an easy smile that seemed to light up even the gloomiest of days, Yajat was a familiar face in his college campus. His dark, expressive eyes held a myriad of emotions, reflecting the depth of his thoughts and the warmth of his personality. From the very first day of college, Yajat had made it his mission to immerse himself in every aspect of campus life. Whether it was participating in extracurricular activities or engaging in lively debates during lectures, Yajat approached each day with enthusiasm and zeal. He was not just a passive observer; he was an active participant in shaping his college experience. Despite being surrounded by a sea of new faces, Yajat quickly found camaraderie in his two closest friends, Rohan and Aditya. Together, they formed an inseparable trio, navigating the ups and downs of college life with unwavering support and laughter. Rohan, with his infectious energy and penchant for mischief, brought a sense of spontaneity to their group, while Aditya, the quiet and introspective one, offered sage advice and a listening ear whenever Yajat needed it.

As the years passed by, Yajat and his friends forged unforgettable memories, from late-night study sessions to impromptu road trips and everything in between. They laughed together, cried together, and grew together, forming bonds that would last a lifetime. But now, as the end of their college journey approached, Yajat found himself grappling with a whirlwind of conflicting emotions. The impending farewell season loomed over him like a bittersweet cloud, reminding him of the countless moments he had shared with his friends and the inevitable goodbye that awaited them. Amidst the flurry of farewell preparations and nostalgic reflections, Yajat couldn't help but feel a sense of apprehension about the uncertain future that lay ahead. What would life be like without the familiar faces and comforting routines of college? Would he be able to navigate the challenges of the real world with the same confidence and resilience that he had shown in college? As he pondered these questions, Yajat knew that the upcoming farewell season would be a time of reflection, celebration, and perhaps even a few tears shed in the name of cherished memories. But amidst the uncertainty, one thing remained constant – the bond of friendship that had sustained him throughout his college journey, and the knowledge that no matter where life took him, his friends would always be there by his side.

In the midst of the hustle and bustle of college life, there was one place where Yajat found solace and comfort: Rahul's coffee shop. Nestled in a quaint corner of the bustling city, the aroma of freshly brewed coffee wafted through the air, drawing Yajat in like a moth to a flame. With its cozy ambiance and warm hospitality, the shop felt like a second home to him. As Yajat entered the shop, he was greeted with a familiar sight – Rahul behind the counter, his face lighting up with a grin as he spotted Yajat. "Ah, the usual affogato for you today?" Rahul quipped, already reaching for the espresso machine with practiced ease. Yajat chuckled, taking his usual seat in the corner of the shop. "You know me too well, Rahul. I can't go a day without your heavenly concoction," he replied with a playful grin. The banter between the two friends flowed effortlessly as Rahul expertly prepared Yajat's affogato, the perfect blend of rich espresso and velvety ice cream. With each sip, Yajat felt his worries melt away, replaced by a sense of contentment and peace. Their conversations ranged from light-hearted jokes to deep discussions about life, love, and everything in between. Rahul was more than just a barista – he was a confidant, a sounding board, and a pillar of support for Yajat through the ups and downs of college life. Every evening, without fail, Yajat would make his way to the coffee shop, eager to catch up with Rahul and unwind after a long day of classes and assignments. It had become a cherished ritual for him, a time to escape the chaos of college and simply enjoy the company of a dear friend. As they shared stories and laughter over steaming cups of coffee, Yajat couldn't help but feel grateful for Rahul's presence in his life. In the midst of deadlines and exams, Rahul's shop provided a sanctuary where he could recharge and find inspiration amidst the comforting aroma of freshly brewed coffee. Their friendship was built on a foundation of mutual respect and understanding, a bond that grew stronger with each passing day. Whether it was discussing their dreams and aspirations or simply enjoying each other's company in comfortable silence, Yajat knew that he could always count on Rahul to be there for him.

As Yajat sat in his usual spot at the coffee shop, he couldn't help but notice the familiar faces of the regulars who frequented the cozy establishment. Each person seemed to have their own story, their own reasons for seeking refuge in the comforting embrace of caffeine and camaraderie. He observed the hustle and bustle of the coffee shop, Yajat found himself reflecting on his own journey – the highs and lows, the triumphs and tribulations that had shaped him into the person he was today.

He thought about his past, particularly his tumultuous breakup that had left him shattered and lost. But as he looked around at the bustling coffee shop, surrounded by the comforting hum of conversation and the rich aroma of freshly brewed coffee, Yajat realized how much he had changed since then. He had emerged from the darkness of his past stronger and more resilient, determined to carve out a future for himself that was bright and full of promise. In the midst of his contemplation, Yajat found himself drawn to the present moment – the simple joys of sipping coffee with friends, the laughter and camaraderie that filled the air. He realized that he had found happiness and fulfillment right here in this coffee shop, without relying on anyone else to complete him. Despite the pain of his past, Yajat was determined to forge ahead with unwavering resolve, embracing the opportunities that lay before him and charting his own course in life. He was no longer defined by his past failures or heartaches; instead, he was fueled by a sense of purpose and determination to succeed. As he took a sip of his coffee, Yajat couldn't help but smile at the thought of how far he had come. He was no longer the same person who had been broken by love and disappointment; he was stronger, wiser, and more resilient than ever before. In that moment, Yajat realized that he was truly happy – not because of anyone else, but because of the person he had become. He had learned to find joy and contentment within himself, embracing his flaws and imperfections as part of what made him unique. As he savored the last drops of his coffee, Yajat felt a sense of gratitude. Gratitude for the friends who had stood by him, for the lessons he had learned along the way, and for the simple pleasures of life that brought him so much joy. And as he stepped out into the bustling city streets, Yajat knew that no matter what challenges lay ahead, he would face them head-on with courage and conviction.

CHAPTER II

A MYSTERY UNRAVELS

The December evening air was crisp and cool as Yajat sat in his usual spot at the coffee shop, engaged in lively conversation with Rahul. As they sipped their coffee and exchanged banter, Rahul broached a topic that Yajat had long avoided – love. Rahul, ever the optimist and well-meaning friend, encouraged Yajat to open up about his feelings and consider moving on from the past. He spoke of the importance of letting go and embracing new opportunities, even suggesting that Yajat might find someone special if he allowed himself to be open to it. But Yajat, stubborn and steadfast in his reluctance to revisit the painful memories of his past relationship, brushed off Rahul's well-intentioned advice. Love was a topic he preferred to steer clear of, preferring instead to focus on his own personal growth and independence. As Rahul prepared another round of coffee, he mentioned in passing that a girl had been asking about Yajat. The mention of this piqued Yajat's interest momentarily, but he quickly dismissed it, shaking his head with a wry smile.

"I'm not interested in entertaining the idea of romance right now, Rahul," Yajat replied, his tone firm and resolute. "I have other priorities in my life, and love isn't one of them."

Rahul nodded understandingly, though he couldn't help but feel a pang of concern for his friend. He knew that Yajat had been through a lot in the past, but he also believed that everyone deserved a second chance at happiness.

"I understand, Yajat," Rahul said, his voice tinged with empathy. "But sometimes, love has a way of finding us when we least expect it. Maybe it's worth considering, even if just for a moment."

Yajat sighed, running a hand through his hair as he contemplated Rahul's words. He knew that his friend meant well, but the wounds of his past relationship were still fresh, and he wasn't sure if he was ready to risk getting hurt again.

"I appreciate your concern, Rahul," Yajat replied, his voice tinged with a hint of sadness. "But for now, I think I'll stick to enjoying my coffee and focusing on myself. Love can wait."

With that, the conversation turned to lighter topics, and Yajat and Rahul spent the rest of the evening laughing and joking as they always did. But deep down, Yajat couldn't shake the feeling that perhaps Rahul was right – that love was something worth considering, even if it meant stepping out of his comfort zone. As the evening drew to a close and Yajat bid farewell to Rahul, he couldn't help but feel a sense of uncertainty lingering in the air. The mention of the mysterious girl who had inquired about him had stirred something within him, a flicker of curiosity that he couldn't quite extinguish. But for now, Yajat pushed aside thoughts of love and romance, choosing instead to focus on the present moment and the simple pleasures of life. As he made his way home, he couldn't help but wonder what the future held in store – and whether love would find him when the time was right.

The days passed by in a blur for Yajat, each one seemingly identical to the last as he immersed himself in his studies and routines. Despite Rahul's persistent mentions of the mysterious girl who had been asking about him, Yajat remained steadfast in his resolve to keep his heart guarded, unwilling to risk the pain of another failed relationship. But one fine morning, as Yajat sat in his college classroom, engrossed in giving a presentation, his phone began to buzz incessantly in his pocket, disrupting his concentration. Glancing down at the screen, he saw multiple missed calls from Rahul, each one bearing an urgency that made his heart race with concern. Unable to answer the calls at that moment, Yajat made a mental note to check in with Rahul later in the evening. As soon as his classes ended for the day, he hurried to the familiar coffee shop where Rahul worked, his mind buzzing with questions about what could have prompted such urgency from his friend.

Upon reaching the coffee shop, Yajat found Rahul behind the counter, his expression a mix of relief and agitation as he spotted his friend approaching.

"Yajat, there you are!" Rahul exclaimed, his voice tinged with urgency. "I've been trying to reach you all morning. The girl, she was here again."

Yajat's heart skipped a beat at the mention of the girl, his curiosity piqued despite his best efforts to remain indifferent. "What girl?" he asked, trying to keep his voice steady.

"The one who's been asking about you," Rahul replied, his eyes searching Yajat's face for any hint of recognition. "She's been coming here quite frequently lately, asking about you. I couldn't ignore it this time, Yajat. I had to call you."

Yajat felt a wave of conflicting emotions wash over him – curiosity, apprehension, and a hint of longing that he couldn't quite shake. Part of him wanted to brush off the topic as unnecessary, to retreat back into the safety of his carefully constructed walls. But another part of him, buried deep beneath the layers of self-preservation, yearned for connection and companionship.

"I appreciate your concern, Rahul," Yajat said, his voice softening with gratitude. "But I'm not sure if I'm ready to entertain the idea of meeting this girl. My past... it's complicated."

Rahul nodded understandingly, his gaze unwavering as he met Yajat's eyes. "I understand, Yajat. But sometimes, we have to take a leap of faith, even if it means risking getting hurt. You can't keep shutting people out because of your past. It's not fair to yourself – or to them." Yajat felt a pang of guilt at Rahul's words, a reminder of the barriers he had erected around his heart in an effort to protect himself from further pain. But he also knew that Rahul was right – that true happiness could only be found by opening oneself up to the possibility of love and connection.

"Okay , I understand, Just take this. She left it for you!", said Rahul.

As Yajat unfolded the note handed to him by Rahul, his eyes widened in surprise at the name written on it – Swarnima. It was a name both distinct and familiar, stirring something deep within him that he couldn't quite place. For a brief moment, his heart skipped a beat as memories and emotions threatened to resurface, but he quickly quelled them, pushing them back behind the protective walls he had built around his heart.

Closing the note with a sense of determination, Yajat looked up to meet Rahul's expectant gaze, his mind racing with conflicting thoughts and emotions. "Swarnima," he murmured, the name lingering on his lips like a forgotten melody. "It's an intriguing name."

Rahul smiled knowingly, sensing the turmoil brewing within his friend. "I understand, Yajat," he said, his voice gentle and reassuring. "Take your time. There's no rush. But promise me you'll at least consider meeting her someday."

Yajat nodded, grateful for Rahul's understanding and support. "I promise, Rahul," he replied, his tone earnest. "For you, I'll keep an open mind. But I need some time to sort things out in my mind first."

Rahul's smile widened at Yajat's words, a sense of relief washing over him. "That's all I ask, my friend," he said, his voice filled with genuine warmth. "I just want to see you happy."

With a shared understanding between them, Yajat and Rahul returned to their usual routine at the coffee shop, the atmosphere tinged with a sense of anticipation and possibility. As Yajat sat sipping his affogato, his mind wandered back to the enigmatic Swarnima, her name echoing in his thoughts like a silent refrain. Taking a deep breath, Yajat made a decision – a decision to step out of his comfort zone and embrace the unknown, whatever it may bring. With Rahul's encouragement and support, he resolved to meet the mysterious girl who had been asking about him, willing to take a chance on love once again. As he left the coffee shop that evening, Yajat felt a sense of nervous anticipation fluttering in his chest, mingled with a newfound sense of hope. Perhaps, just perhaps, this unexpected encounter would mark the beginning of a new chapter in his life – one filled with possibility, growth, and the potential for love.

CHAPTER III

BREAKING BARRIERS

Time passed, and Yajat found himself engrossed in the whirlwind of his college life. Days blended into weeks as he juggled lectures, assignments, and late-night study sessions. In the midst of his hectic routine, he seldom spared a thought for the note from Swarnima, though he had carefully tucked it away in his diary. It was a constant reminder of something he wasn't quite ready to confront. Despite his reluctance, Rahul never gave up. He would gently nudge Yajat, reminding him that there was someone out there who genuinely wanted to meet him. "Just give it a chance, Yajat," Rahul would say, his tone a blend of encouragement and exasperation. "What's the harm in meeting her once?" Respecting his best friend's persistence and knowing that Rahul only had his best interests at heart, Yajat finally agreed to meet Swarnima, albeit half-heartedly. He wasn't entirely convinced it was the right decision, but for Rahul, he was willing to give it a try.

One evening, as he sat at his desk, the diary lay open before him. His eyes fell on the note from Swarnima, and for the first time in weeks, he picked it up. He read her words again: "Please let us meet once – Swarnima." A wave of uncertainty overtook over him, and he found himself contemplating his past, the source of his hesitations. As he read the note over and over, his thoughts drifted back to the last relationship that had left him guarded and wary. The memories were still fresh, the pain still real. He closed his eyes, the note slipping from his fingers as he leaned back in his chair, lost in thought. Sleep crept up on him, and he found himself dreaming. In his dream, he imagined a girl dressed in traditional attire, a delicate bindi adorning her forehead and jhumkas swaying gently with each movement. Her eyes were mesmerizing, holding a depth that drew him in. The image was so vivid, so captivating, that it felt almost real. He envisioned their first meeting at a quaint coffee shop, her smile lighting up the room as she spoke in a soft, melodic voice. The dream was everything he had ever hoped for, a perfect blend of charm and elegance. But reality shattered his dream as his phone buzzed loudly, jolting him awake. His heart raced as he glanced at the screen, seeing Rahul's name flashing. For a moment, he felt a pang of disappointment, the beautiful vision of Swarnima lingering in his mind, making the prospect of meeting her in real life feel daunting. High expectations had been set by his dream, and he feared that reality might not measure up.

"Hey, Rahul," Yajat answered, trying to steady his

voice.

"Hey, buddy. Are you ready for tonight?" Rahul's voice was cheerful, yet there was an underlying tone of urgency.

"Yeah, I guess," Yajat replied, his hesitation evident.

"Great! Don't overthink it, okay? Just be yourself. She's really looking forward to meeting you," Rahul encouraged.

With a sigh, Yajat ended the call and reluctantly began to get ready. He chose a simple yet neat outfit, hoping to make a good impression without drawing too much attention to himself. His mind was a whirlwind of emotions – excitement, nervousness, and a lingering doubt.

As the evening descended, Yajat found himself at the familiar coffee shop. The warm, inviting aroma of freshly brewed coffee filled the air, and he made his way to his favorite corner seat. He sat down, the familiar ambiance bringing a semblance of comfort amid his swirling thoughts. He ordered his usual affogato and waited, his mind replaying the dream and contrasting it with the uncertainties of reality. His heart was encompassing a string of hopes and fears, the weight of his past holding him back even as he yearned for something new. Minutes ticked by, and Yajat's anticipation grew. Each time the door opened, his eyes darted towards it, wondering if the next person to walk-in would-be Swarnima. He was lost in a sea of thoughts, his nerves getting the better of him. Swarnima entered the coffee shop, her eyes scanning the room until they landed on Yajat. As she walked toward him, Yajat's heart sank a little. She was nothing like the girl in his dreams – no traditional attire, no bindi, no mesmerizing eyes. Instead, she was dressed casually, her hair tied back, looking like any other girl one might see on the street. Yajat cursed his mind for building up such unrealistic expectations.

Despite his disappointment, Yajat knew he couldn't let it ruin the evening. He forced a smile and stood up to greet her. "Hi, I'm Yajat," he said, extending his hand.

"Hi, I'm Swarnima," she replied, shaking his hand with a warm smile. She took the seat across from him, and they settled into an awkward silence for a moment.

"So, what do you do in your free time?" Swarnima asked, breaking the ice.

"Well, I like writing," Yajat replied, his voice gaining a bit of confidence. "And I'm a big cricket fan. I play whenever I get the chance."

Swarnima's eyes lit up. "That's interesting! What do you write about?"

"Mostly short stories and some poetry," Yajat said. "It's a way for me to express my thoughts and feelings."

"That's amazing," Swarnima said, genuinely impressed. "I've always admired people who can write. I'm more of an explorer myself. I love traveling to new places and experiencing different cultures."

Yajat nodded, intrigued despite himself. "That sounds exciting. Do you have a favorite place you've visited?"

"Hmm, that's a tough one," Swarnima replied, thinking for a moment. "I'd say the mountains. There's something so serene and peaceful about them. They make me feel alive."

They continued their small talk, gradually growing more comfortable with each other. Yajat found himself warming up to Swarnima, even though she wasn't what he had envisioned. She was genuine and interesting, and he could see why Rahul had insisted on him meeting her.

After a while, Yajat decided to address the question that had been on his mind since he first heard about her. "Swarnima, I have to ask – why were you so persistent about meeting me?"

Swarnima smiled, a hint of amusement in her eyes. "Honestly? Your name caught my attention. It's quite unique. And I felt like making a new connection. I believe in following my instincts, and something about you intrigued me."

Yajat couldn't help but chuckle. "Well, I'm glad you did. It's been nice talking to you."

Swarnima's smile widened. "I'm glad too. Sometimes, the best connections come from the most unexpected places."

They continued their conversation, discussing their favorite books, movies, and places they wanted to visit. Yajat found himself genuinely enjoying Swarnima's company. She was easy to talk to, and her adventurous spirit was infectious. Despite the initial disappointment, he realized that meeting her was turning out to be a pleasant experience.

Although the meeting was going smoothly, Yajat knew that the dreaded question might come up. And within a moment, Swarnima asked, "Why were you so reluctant to meet? Why did you avoid me so much? Even the note I sent for you was weeks back? Any specific reason?"

Yajat couldn't answer this. He had too much of his past to deal with, but it wasn't Swarnima who caused it all. Telling her would be burdening her with his problems. Finding the right reason to articulate, they sat in silence. The seconds dragged on, and Yajat could feel the weight of the question hanging heavily between them. Just then, Rahul called him over to the counter for the bill as the shop's system had to be logged off for the day. Yajat felt a surge of relief. "Excuse me for a moment," he said to Swarnima, grateful for the escape. He walked to the counter, hoping the distraction would diffuse the tension. While fetching the cash, a few petals of dried roses fell from his wallet. Both he and Rahul knew what it meant. The roses were a remnant of his past relationship, a painful reminder of the heartbreak he had endured. Swarnima glanced at the petals, her eyes curious yet understanding.

Rahul quickly tried to handle the situation casually. "Yajat, just leave it and move on," he said, trying to sound light-hearted but failing to hide his concern. This was fuel to Yajat's already racing mind. He couldn't handle it anymore.

Yajat gave a stern look to Rahul, feeling a rush of emotions he couldn't control. Without a moment's hesitation, he decided he needed to get out of there. He returned to Swarnima, trying to mask his inner turmoil. "I'm sorry, Swarnima, but I have to leave now. Something urgent came up," he said abruptly.

Swarnima looked taken aback but nodded understandingly. "It's okay, Yajat. Take care."

He hurriedly left the shop, mumbling a quick goodbye to Rahul. As he walked back to his hostel, his mind was a mess. The memories of his past relationship, Swarnima's questions, and the sight of the dried rose petals all swirled in his head. It was too much for him to bear. He couldn't face it all again. Back in his hostel room, Yajat felt exhausted. He tossed his wallet on the table and collapsed onto his bed. The events of the evening played over and over in his mind, each detail more vivid than the last. He thought about Swarnima, her curiosity, and how she had been persistent yet respectful. He regretted not being able to be honest with her. But the sight of the dried rose petals brought back too many memories. His last relationship had ended in heartbreak, and he had built walls around himself to prevent such pain from happening again. Swarnima's genuine interest and questions had poked at those walls, and he wasn't ready to let them come down. He lay in bed, staring at the ceiling, trying to push the thoughts away. His mind, however, refused to cooperate. He thought about Rahul's words, urging him to move on. He knew Rahul was right, but the fear of getting hurt again was too overwhelming. Eventually, fatigue took over, and Yajat felt his eyes grow heavy. He welcomed the oblivion of sleep, hoping that it would offer some respite from the chaos in his mind. As he drifted off, he tried to convince himself that today was just a bad dream, something he could forget about in the morning. His last conscious thought was of Swarnima, her smile, and the curiosity in her eyes. He hoped she wouldn't give up on him entirely, but for now, he needed to find peace within himself. With that, Yajat finally succumbed to sleep, his mind a turbulent sea gradually calming under the soothing waves of unconsciousness.

CHAPTER IV

The Palpable Tension

Weeks had passed since the turbulent encounter with Swarnima. Despite Yajat's wish to avoid her, Swarnima was persistent. Each morning, her messages would light up his phone with a cheerful "Good morning!" She would call him to chit-chat, trying to bridge the gap between them. Yajat found it exhausting. This was charted territory for him, territory he had no intention of revisiting.

His responses to Swarnima were always curt, his tone cold. He avoided her calls when he could, and when he did answer, their conversations were brief and devoid of warmth. His walls were firmly up, and he was determined to keep them that way.

One evening, as Yajat sat in his favorite corner at Rahul's coffee shop, sipping his usual affogato, Rahul watched him closely. Rahul had been observing Yajat's behavior for weeks, noticing the growing distance between his friend and Swarnima. He could see the pain Yajat was causing himself, and it troubled him deeply.

Rahul decided it was time to intervene. He approached Yajat and sat down across from him, his expression serious. "Yajat, we need to talk."

Yajat looked up, surprised by Rahul's tone. "What's up, Rahul?"

Rahul took a deep breath. "It's about Swarnima. I've noticed how you've been treating her. You're avoiding her, keeping her at arm's length. This isn't like you."

Yajat sighed, rubbing his temples. "I just... I don't want to get involved, Rahul. You know my past. I can't go through that again."

"I get it, man. But Swarnima isn't asking for anything more than friendship. She's reaching out, trying to make a connection, and you're shutting her out."

"Rahul, I'm scared. I don't want to get hurt again," Yajat admitted, his voice barely above a whisper.

Rahul leaned forward, his eyes earnest. "Look, Yajat, I understand your fear. But living like this, closed off and isolated, isn't healthy. You're not just hurting yourself; you're hurting Swarnima too. She doesn't deserve this."

Yajat stared at his friend, feeling a mix of guilt and confusion. "What should I do, Rahul? How do I move past this?"

Rahul placed a comforting hand on Yajat's shoulder. "Start by being honest with her. Let her know you value her effort to be your friend. It's a step, Yajat. Just take it one step at a time."

Yajat nodded slowly, realizing the truth in Rahul's words. "I've been so wrong, haven't I?"

Rahul smiled gently. "We all make mistakes, Yajat. What matters is that you're willing to make things right."

That night, Yajat lay in bed, reflecting on his conversation with Rahul. He knew he had to face his fears and confront his true self. Swarnima had done nothing wrong; she was merely looking for a friend. And he had been shutting her out, letting his past dictate his present.

The next morning, Yajat woke up with a sense of determination. He picked up his phone and saw the usual "Good morning!" message from Swarnima. This time, he responded with more than a terse reply.

"Good morning, Swarnima. I hope you have a great day. Can we talk later?"

He sent the message and felt a sense of relief. It was a small step, but it was a start. He needed to apologize, to explain his behavior, and to make amends. Despite his reluctance, Yajat found himself slowly opening up to Swarnima. She was persistent, never letting a chance to connect slip by. Their conversations, once terse and guarded, began to flow more naturally. It started with simple messages and evolved into longer phone calls. Swarnima's cheerful voice became a regular part of his evenings, a comforting presence he hadn't realized he missed.

One afternoon, after a particularly engaging conversation about their favorite books, Swarnima's voice took on a hopeful tone. "Yajat, would you like to meet this evening? Maybe we can grab a coffee or something."

Caught off guard, Yajat's old instincts kicked in. He

hesitated, his mind racing with excuses. "I... I'm really sorry, Swarnima, but I have plans this evening," he lied, his voice sounding more strained than he intended. He quickly ended the call, the guilt settling in almost immediately.

The moment he hung up, it hit him how wrong he had been. His stomach churned with regret, and he could feel the walls he had carefully built around his heart start to crumble. He realized he had done exactly what he promised himself he wouldn't do: he let fear dictate his actions. Without giving himself time to second-guess, he grabbed his phone and called Swarnima back.

"Swarnima," he began, his voice more earnest than before, "I'm really sorry. I lied. I don't have plans. I just... I got nervous."

There was a brief silence on the other end before Swarnima's voice came through, gentle and understanding. "It's okay, Yajat. I understand. How about we do something simple? Would you like to go to a movie? There's a good one playing at 5 PM."

Yajat felt a wave of relief. She wasn't angry or hurt; she just wanted to spend time with him. "Yes, that sounds great. I'd love to go."

As he ended the call, Yajat felt a lightness he hadn't felt in years. He was genuinely happy, not just for agreeing to the movie, but for finally allowing himself to step out of his self-imposed isolation. He was giving Swarnima the chance she deserved, and in doing so, he was giving himself a chance to heal and move forward. The rest of the day, he couldn't help but feel a mixture of excitement and nervousness. He was looking forward to the evening, to the movie, and to spending time with Swarnima. It was a new experience, one that signified a break from his past and the beginning of something hopeful.

When 5 PM approached, Yajat found himself getting ready with a level of care he hadn't taken in a long time. As he walked to the movie theater, he felt a surge of anticipation. This was different, and he was ready to embrace it. For the first time in a long while, Yajat felt like he was taking control of his life, stepping into a future where he allowed himself to be happy, to form new connections. And with Swarnima by his side, he felt that maybe, just maybe, he was on the right path. Yajat and Swarnima settled into their seats as the theater lights dimmed. The trailers played, and Yajat began to notice a sinking feeling in his stomach. When the main feature began, his heart sank further. It was a romantic Hollywood movie—a genre he had always found uncomfortable, one he had tried to avoid. He shifted in his seat, the reluctance he felt towards Hollywood films resurfacing. He glanced at Swarnima, who was watching the screen with an eager expression, and tried to mask his discomfort.

But his unease must have been palpable, because Swarnima turned to him with a concerned look. "Yajat, what's the matter? You seem really uncomfortable."

Yajat hesitated, caught between wanting to be honest and not wanting to ruin the evening for Swarnima. Finally, he sighed. "I'm not really a fan of Hollywood romantic movies," he confessed. "They've just never been my thing."

Swarnima's expression softened with understanding. "We don't have to stay if you don't want to. I don't want you to be uncomfortable."

Yajat quickly shook his head. "No, let's stay. I want to be here with you. It's just...I'm not used to this."

There was an eerie silence between them as they continued to watch the movie. Yajat tried to focus on the screen, but his mind kept wandering. He felt like he was letting Swarnima down, and the thought gnawed at him. After a while, Swarnima broke the silence with a question that cut through his thoughts.

"Yajat, tell me honestly. Am I disturbing you? I just want to make a genuine connection, but you seem different. Please, do tell me if you want me to leave."

Her words hit him like a ton of bricks. Yajat felt a wave of guilt drowning him. He realized how his reluctance and discomfort might have come across to Swarnima. He turned to her, his eyes earnest and apologetic.

"Swarnima, it's not you. My mind is just a mess because of my past. I've built these walls to protect myself, and sometimes it's hard to let them down," he admitted. "I was reluctant to meet you at first, but that's not because of anything you did. It's because of me. But I genuinely enjoy our friendship, and I want to keep it. I'm sorry if I've made you feel otherwise."

Swarnima listened quietly, her eyes softening as he spoke. She reached out and gently squeezed his hand. "I understand, Yajat. Thank you for telling me. I'm here for you, and I'm glad we're friends."

Her words brought a sense of relief to Yajat. He could see that Swarnima wasn't upset with him, and that made all the difference. He decided then and there that he would make a concerted effort to be more selfless, to cherish the connections he was making without letting his past hold him back. As the movie progressed, Swarnima got engrossed in the story, and Yajat tried to do the same. He found himself smiling at the occasional funny scenes and even feeling a bit moved by the romantic moments, despite his initial reluctance. He realized that sometimes stepping out of his comfort zone was necessary to grow and to build meaningful relationships.

As the movie progressed, Yajat tried his best to focus on the screen, but his mind kept drifting back to Swarnima sitting beside him. He couldn't shake off the unease that had settled in his chest since they entered the theater. Then, out of the blue, Swarnima shifted closer to him and rested her head on his shoulder. At first, Yajat froze, his heart pounding in his chest. He felt a surge of panic rise within him, threatening to engulf him in memories he had tried so hard to bury. The weight of her head on his shoulder felt like a trigger, pulling him back into the past he had fought so hard to leave behind. But then he looked at Swarnima, her eyes fixed on the screen, completely unaware of the turmoil raging within him. He saw nothing but innocence and genuine warmth in her gesture. She was seeking comfort, nothing more. It wasn't fair to let his past dictate his present, to push away someone who had done nothing but show him kindness.

Taking a deep breath, Yajat made a conscious effort to push aside his intrusive thoughts. He reminded himself of his determination to be selfless, to embrace the connections he was forging without letting his past hold him back. Slowly, tentatively, he relaxed his tense muscles and allowed Swarnima to rest her head on his shoulder. For the remainder of the movie, Yajat felt a mixture of emotions swirling within him—fear, uncertainty, but also a strange sense of peace. Swarnima's presence beside him was both comforting and unsettling, a reminder of the internal battles he still had to fight. When the credits finally rolled and the lights came back on, Yajat turned to Swarnima, offering her a small smile. "Thank you for staying for me," she said softly, her eyes full of gratitude. Yajat returned her smile, feeling a weight lift off his shoulders. "Of course," he replied, his voice steady despite the turmoil still simmering beneath the surface. "I'm glad I could be here for you." With a sense of finality, they stood up from their seats and made their way out of the theater. Swarnima thanked him again, her words echoing in his mind as they said their goodbyes. As they parted ways, Yajat couldn't help but feel a glimmer of hope flicker within him. Maybe, just maybe, he could learn to let go of the past and embrace the future with Swarnima by his side. With a side hug, he showed his belief and determination to forge this bond, even if it meant facing his deepest fears head-on. As they went their separate ways, Yajat couldn't shake off the feeling that this was just the beginning of something new and beautiful.

CHAPTER V

BOND BEYOND WORDS

As the days became weeks, Yajat found himself growing increasingly accustomed to Swarnima's presence in his life. What had started as a tentative friendship had blossomed into something deeper and more meaningful. Yajat now took the initiative to text Swarnima good morning, eager to start the day with her warm and comforting presence. Their bond had become healthier and more vibrant, with each passing day bringing them closer together. They would chat for hours on video calls, exchanging stories, sharing laughter, and delving into deep conversations late into the night. Yajat found solace in Swarnima's company, her gentle demeanor and caring nature providing him with a sense of comfort and stability that he hadn't known before. Although Yajat still hesitated to anything more than friendship, he couldn't deny the strong attachment he felt towards Swarnima. She had become an integral part of his daily life, a constant presence that he found himself relying on more and more with each passing day. Their conversations were not just limited to idle chatter; they would often discuss their plans for the day, sharing outfit ideas and fashion tips. Swarnima would suggest new places for Yajat to explore, introducing him to hidden gems and local hotspots that he had never even heard of before. Her enthusiasm for life was infectious, and Yajat found himself eager to experience new adventures with her by his side. Despite his growing feelings, Yajat remained cautious, unwilling to rush into anything that he wasn't ready for. He cherished the friendship that he had with Swarnima and was afraid of jeopardizing it by crossing any boundaries. Yet, with each passing day, he found himself drawn to her in ways that he couldn't fully understand. Their late-night talks became a highlight of Yajat's day, a time when he could let down his guard and be himself without fear of judgment or rejection. Swarnima had a way of making him feel seen and understood, and he found himself opening up to her in ways that he had never done with anyone else before. Yajat couldn't deny the undeniable chemistry that existed between them. Swarnima had a way of making him feel alive, of bringing color and joy into his otherwise monotonous existence.

Yajat and Swarnima's growing bond couldn't go unnoticed by their respective friends. As they introduced each other to their social circles, Yajat's friends couldn't help but tease him mercilessly about his newfound connection with Swarnima. They would nudge him, exchange knowing looks, and make playful remarks that never failed to make Yajat blush. It had been a long time since Yajat's friends had seen this side of him – the shy, slightly awkward side that came out whenever he was around someone he cared about. But despite the teasing, they could see how happy Yajat was, and they were genuinely happy for him. They had watched him struggle with his emotions in the past, and seeing him finally find someone who brought out the best in him was a cause for celebration. Swarnima, too, introduced Yajat to her friends, and the reception was equally warm. Yajat found himself welcomed into Swarnima's social circle with open arms, and he couldn't help but feel grateful for the kindness and acceptance he received from her friends. They were a diverse group, each bringing their own unique energy and personality to the table, and Yajat enjoyed getting to know them and learning more about Swarnima's life outside of their own little bubble. They laughed off the teasing and embraced the support and encouragement that their friends offered. It was a refreshing change of pace for Yajat, who had spent so long keeping his emotions bottled up inside, afraid to let anyone get too close. But with Swarnima by his side, Yajat felt like he could finally be himself, unapologetically and unabashedly. He revelled in the laughter, the camaraderie, and the sense of belonging that he found in both their social circles, grateful for the newfound sense of joy and fulfillment that Swarnima had brought into his life. And with each passing day, their bond only grew stronger, fortified by the love, laughter, and unbreakable friendship that they shared.

Yajat found himself developing a strange but powerful protective instinct towards Swarnima. He couldn't help but feel a surge of anger and jealousy whenever he noticed her being careless or neglecting her well-being. If she forgot to eat or pushed herself too hard, Yajat would feel a pang of worry and frustration, unable to shake the feeling that he needed to watch over her and keep her safe. It wasn't just about wanting Swarnima to be happy – although that was certainly a big part of it. For Yajat, it was also about cherishing the connection they shared and making the most of the time they had together in college. He knew that their time was limited, and he was determined to make every moment count.

So whenever he saw Swarnima getting caught up in the whirlwind of college life – staying out late, partying too hard, or neglecting her health – Yajat couldn't help but feel a surge of protectiveness. He wanted to shield her from harm, to be her rock and her anchor in a sea of uncertainty and chaos. It was a strange feeling for Yajat, who had always prided himself on being independent and self-sufficient. But with Swarnima, he found himself willingly setting aside his own needs and desires in favor of hers. He was willing to go to great lengths to ensure her happiness and well-being, even if it meant sacrificing his own comfort or peace of mind in the process. And while part of him knew that his protective instincts might come across as overbearing or intrusive at times, he couldn't help but act on them. He cared deeply for Swarnima, and he couldn't bear the thought of anything happening to her on his watch. So he continued to watch over her, silently and steadfastly, always ready to lend a helping hand or offer a word of advice when she needed it most. And in return, Swarnima showered him with gratitude and affection, grateful for the unwavering support and care that he provided. Together, their bond grew stronger with each passing day. But amidst the warmth and affection, a bittersweet realization lingered in Yajat's mind – their time together in college was drawing to a close. With the farewell day fast approaching, Yajat couldn't help but feel a twinge of sadness at the thought of leaving behind the place where he had forged such meaningful connections. But as he prepared to bid farewell to his college days, Yajat resolved to cherish every moment, knowing that the memories he had made would stay with him forever.

CHAPTER VI

FAREWELL'S KISS

The day of farewell had finally arrived after month of happy experiences and new connections, and Yajat's heart was a swirl of mixed emotions. He stood in front of the mirror, savoring each moment as he got dressed for this significant day. He chose his favorite black formals, the crisp lines of the suit accentuating his tall frame. But amidst the sentimentality, there was also a sense of readiness to embrace the new phase of life that awaited him beyond these college walls. Once he was fully dressed, Yajat reached for his phone. It was time for his customary video call with Swarnima. The screen lit up with her smiling face, and he felt a warm comfort in her presence, even through the digital screen.

Swarnima laughed softly. "You look perfect, Yajat. Ready for the big day?"

Yajat nodded, though his smile carried a hint of

sadness. "Yeah, ready as I'll ever be. It's just... a lot to take in."

"I know," Swarnima said, her tone gentle. "But remember, this is just the beginning of new adventures. You'll do great."

With her words echoing in his mind, Yajat ended the call. He took a deep breath, squared his shoulders, and stepped out of his room, ready to face the day. Each step down the familiar hallways was a walk through memories, each corner holding a story. As he approached the auditorium, where the farewell ceremony would be held, Yajat's emotions were a complex mix of excitement and melancholy. Every handshake, hug, and smile seemed to take a bit longer, as if everyone was savoring these final moments together. The auditorium doors loomed ahead, a threshold between the past and the future.

The farewell was a joyful, bittersweet celebration of their time together. The auditorium buzzed with excitement as everyone gathered for one last time. Friends greeted each other with wide smiles, laughter echoing through the hall. There was a palpable sense of nostalgia in the air as groups huddled, discussing their future plans, reminiscing about shared experiences, and making promises to stay in touch. Yajat, dressed in his black formals, looked around, taking in the vibrant atmosphere. It was a day of mixed emotions, a day of endings and new beginnings. The highlight came when Yajat was rightfully crowned Mr. Farewell. Cheers erupted, and Yajat felt a surge of pride and happiness. Yajat smiled, his eyes meeting those of his friends and classmates. He observed the bonds being strengthened, promises being made. He couldn't help but reflect on his own journey, realizing how much he had grown over the years. The day was a whirlwind of activities, from dancing and singing to heartfelt speeches and group photos. Yajat found himself in deep conversations, light-hearted banter, and even silent moments of reflection. The farewell was not just a goodbye but a celebration of their collective journey, a testament to the bonds they had forged. As the day progressed, Yajat barely noticed how quickly time was flying. It wasn't until the sun began to set that he realized the day was coming to an end. The reality of saying final goodbyes to his classmates began to sink in. He felt a lump in his throat as he embraced each friend, expressing gratitude and wishing them well. It was an emotional experience, each goodbye a reminder of the precious times they had shared. There were tears, laughter, and heartfelt words exchanged.

As the farewell drew to a close Yajat knew it was time to move on to the hardest part of saying goodbye. With a heavy heart, he made his way to meet Rahul, his closest friend and confidant. Yajat walked slowly toward the coffee shop; each step filled with the weight of finality. The coffee shop had been a second home to him, a place of comfort and camaraderie, all thanks to Rahul. As he entered, the familiar aroma of freshly brewed coffee greeted him, but today, it felt different, more poignant. Rahul, busy behind the counter, looked up and immediately sensed the gravity of the moment. He came around the counter, and without a word, they embraced. The hug was long and filled with unspoken emotions, each pat on the back a testament to their deep bond. When they finally pulled apart, their eyes were misty, but their smiles were genuine.

"Let's sit," Yajat said, not asking for his usual coffee

this time. He just wanted Rahul by his side, as he had been for all these years.

They found a quiet corner and settled into the plush chairs. Yajat took a deep breath, gathering his thoughts. "Rahul, I don't think I can ever thank you enough for everything you've done for me," he began, his voice tinged with emotion. "You've been more than a friend, more than a brother."

Rahul smiled warmly. "You've been the same for me, Yajat. These years wouldn't have been the same without you."

"I'll miss this place," Yajat admitted, looking around the coffee shop. "But more than that, I'll miss you, Rahul. You've been a constant in my life, and it's hard to imagine not seeing you every day."

Rahul nodded, feeling the same bittersweet mix of emotions. "I'll miss you too, Yajat. But remember, this isn't goodbye. We may not see each other every day, but our friendship will always be there."

Yajat felt a sense of comfort in Rahul's words. "You're right. This isn't goodbye, just a new chapter." Yajat and Rahul's heartfelt conversation was suddenly interrupted by the soft chime of the coffee shop door opening. Yajat looked up and saw Swarnima standing there, a hesitant smile on her face. Rahul, ever perceptive, gave Yajat a knowing look. "I'll give you two some space," he said, patting Yajat on the shoulder before discreetly retreating behind the counter.

Swarnima walked over to where Yajat was sitting. He stood up, greeting her with a warm smile. "Hey," he said softly, pulling out a chair for her.

"I'm glad you came," Yajat said, breaking the silence. "I wanted to talk to you."

Swarnima's eyes softened. "I'm glad I came too. I

wasn't sure if you'd want to see me after everything."

Yajat shook his head. "No, it's not like that. I've been thinking a lot, and I realize now how much you mean to me. We've only known each other for just a few months, but it feels like we've shared a lifetime of memories."

Swarnima smiled, her eyes glistening with unshed tears. "I feel the same way. You've become such an important part of my life, Yajat."

Swarnima squeezed his hand, her expression turning more serious. "But what happens now? Is this the final goodbye?"

Yajat sighed, feeling the weight of her question. "It does seem like it," he admitted. "I have a flight to catch tomorrow, and I don't know where destiny might take me."

Hearing this, Swarnima's face fell, the sadness in her eyes making Yajat's heart ache. He hadn't meant to hurt her, but the thought of leaving her behind was more painful than he had anticipated.

Seeing her so visibly sad made Yajat's resolve weaken. "Let's not think about it as a goodbye," he said, trying to sound more hopeful. "We'll stay connected, no matter what."

He didn't want to leave her yet, not with so much still left unsaid. "How about I walk you to your hostel?" he suggested.

Swarnima nodded, a small smile returning to her face. "I'd like that."

They left the coffee shop, walking side by side through the quiet city. The air was cool, and the stars above seemed to shine just a little brighter, as if acknowledging the significance of their moment together. As they approached Swarnima's hostel, the reality of their impending separation hit them both even harder. Neither of them wanted to say goodbye, but they knew they had to. Standing outside the entrance, they turned to face each other.

"Yajat," Swarnima began, her voice trembling slightly, "promise me you'll never forget me. Promise me you'll always stay the same."

Yajat's eyes filled with tears. "I promise," he said, his voice thick with emotion. "I'll never forget you, and I'll always be the same. We'll stay connected, no matter where life takes us."

They embraced, holding each other tightly, not wanting to let go. The world around them seemed to fade away, leaving just the two of them, wrapped in each other's arms. The intensity of their feelings was overwhelming, and in that moment, Yajat knew he had to show Swarnima just how much she meant to him. He pulled back slightly, looking into her eyes. "Swarnima," he whispered, his voice barely audible. Then, before he could second-guess himself, he leaned in and kissed her. It was a kiss filled with all the emotions he had kept bottled up inside—love, fear, hope, and sorrow. Swarnima responded, her arms tightening around him, returning his kiss with equal fervor. It was as if time had stopped, and nothing else mattered but the two of them. When they finally broke apart, both of them had tears streaming down their faces. Without a word, they held each other for a few more moments, savoring the closeness. Then, knowing it was time, they reluctantly let go. Yajat watched as Swarnima turned and walked into her hostel, her figure disappearing into the shadows.

As he made his way back to his own hostel, Yajat felt a mix of emotions swirling inside him. He was sad, yes, but also strangely at peace. He had faced his fears, embraced his connection with Swarnima, and given her a piece of his heart. It wasn't the ending he had envisioned, but it was an ending nonetheless. Back in his room, as he closed his eyes, he felt a sense of calm. Whatever lay ahead, he was ready to face it, knowing that he had made a lifelong connection that would stay with him forever.

CHAPTER VII

ECHOES OF HUSTLE

Yajat woke up to the sound of his alarm at 8 AM. The morning sunlight streamed through the window, casting a warm glow across his room. Today was the day after months of happiness it was finally time to leave. The day he would leave behind his college life and head to Bangalore. A mix of excitement and melancholy filled his heart as he got ready, packing the last of his belongings into his suitcase. He took one final look around his hostel room, every corner filled with memories. His friends were waiting for him in the common area, and they shared a heartfelt goodbye, filled with promises to stay in touch and visit each other. Yajat felt a lump in his throat as he finally walked out of the hostel, each step feeling heavier than the last. The cab ride to the airport was quiet, the city waking up to a new day. About halfway through the journey, his phone buzzed. It was Swarnima. He smiled and answered the video call.

"Hey," she said softly. "Are you on your way?"

"Yeah," Yajat replied, his voice tinged with sadness. "I'm in the cab right now."

They talked about everything and nothing, trying to fill the silence with memories and shared dreams. Swarnima's eyes sparkled with unshed tears, and Yajat felt a lump in his throat.

"Yajat," she said after a pause, "I'm going to miss you so much."

"I'll miss you too, Swarnima," he replied, his voice cracking. "But we'll stay connected, right? This isn't goodbye forever."

She nodded, her smile tremulous. "Yes, we'll stay in touch. Promise me you'll take care of yourself and stay happy."

"I promise," Yajat said, trying to keep his emotions in check. "And you too. Be happy and keep smiling."

As the cab pulled up to the airport, Yajat knew it was time to end the call. "Swarnima, I have to go now. My flight..."

"I know," she interrupted, her voice barely above a whisper. "Take care, Yajat. Safe travels."

"Thank you," he said, his heart aching. "Goodbye, Swarnima."

"Goodbye," she whispered, and with that, the call ended. He got out of the cab, taking his suitcase and heading towards the terminal.

Yajat quickly navigated through the security frisking, moving with a sense of purpose. He sent a quick message to his dad, letting him know he was about to board the flight. The airport buzzed with activity, a symphony of emotions playing out around him. Couples shared tearful goodbyes, families reunited with joyous embraces. These scenes tugged at Yajat's heart, making him think of Swarnima. He wondered how different it might have been if she were here, sharing this moment with him. He boarded the plane, finding his seat and stowing his carry-on. As he settled in, he glanced around at the other passengers. Everywhere, there were people with loved ones, holding hands, exchanging smiles. The sight stirred a longing within him, a desire for Swarnima's presence. Her absence felt like a void, a reminder of the connection they had forged over months of bonding. Taking a deep breath, Yajat closed his eyes and tried to calm his racing thoughts. It wasn't easy to push aside the thoughts of Swarnima, but he knew he needed to focus on the journey ahead. Landing in Bangalore, Yajat felt a surge of determination. He collected his luggage and stepped into the bustling city, ready to face whatever challenges and adventures lay ahead.

Yajat spent the rest of the day lying on his bed, scrolling through the memories stored in his phone. Each photo and video brought back vivid moments from his college days, his friends, and most of all, Swarnima. The ache of missing everything, and her especially, was profound.

He casually called his dad, trying to sound upbeat. "Hey Dad, just letting you know I got here safe," he began.

"Good to hear, son. How's it going so far?" his dad asked, his voice filled with warmth and concern.

"Well, it's okay. Just... not finding it very adjustable here yet. I might move if things don't get better," Yajat admitted, keeping the conversation light. He avoided going into the deeper feelings of displacement and longing that burned at him.

"Give it some time, Yajat. You'll find your rhythm," his dad encouraged.

"Yeah, I hope so," Yajat replied, though he wasn't entirely convinced.

After ending the call, he tried to shake off the lingering melancholy. He knew he had to prepare for the next day. Tomorrow would be his first step towards the new phase of his life. He would be scouting his probable campus and meeting his future professors. This was an opportunity to set a positive tone for his time in Bangalore. As he lay down to sleep, he resolved to embrace the new experiences ahead while keeping the memories of his past close to his heart.

Yajat's first few weeks in Bangalore was a whirlwind of activities and emotions. He scouted several colleges, trying to find the right fit for his further studies. The campuses were impressive, and he met many new people, potential classmates, and professors. Despite the bustling environment and the promising academic opportunities, Yajat felt a persistent void in his heart. Every evening, as he returned to his temporary accommodation, the sense of something missing grew stronger. The only solace came from his nightly video calls with Swarnima. Her presence on the screen was a brief respite from the loneliness that enveloped him in this new city.

One evening, frustrated with the continuous feelings of longings and not being able to handle this unknown city over the past half month, Yajat sat in his room, scrolling through job portals out of sheer habit, something caught his eye. An opening for a research analyst in Delhi, seeking urgent hiring. Yajat's heart skipped a beat. Delhi was closer to everything he missed: his friends, family, and most importantly, Swarnima. The thought of moving back filled him with a sudden rush of hope. Without wasting a moment, he applied for the position, feeling a mix of excitement and nervousness. He decided to keep this a secret from Swarnima, wanting to surprise her if things worked out. Days passed, and Yajat continued his routine of college visits and video calls. One morning, lost in all the hustle of his new life, he received an email inviting him for an interview. His heart raced as he prepared for it, carefully selecting his attire and rehearsing answers to potential questions. The interview went smoothly, and by the end, he felt confident. His anticipation grew as he awaited their decision. The wait for the mail of selection made him impatient but alas, Yajat received the news he had been longing for: he had cleared the interview, and his joining date was set for next month. His excitement was boundless. He called his family to share the news, and they were supportive, though not surprised. Changing plans and following his heart was typical for Yajat, and they were happy to see him take a step towards what he truly wanted.

As the days passed, Yajat could barely contain his elation. The thought of surprising Swarnima filled him with joy. He imagined the look on her face when he told her he was coming back. His stay in Bangalore had been a rollercoaster of emotions, but it had ultimately strengthened his bond with Swarnima. On the night before his departure, Yajat sat in his room, packing his bags with a sense of purpose and anticipation. He neatly folded his clothes, packed his books, and gathered his essentials, all the while thinking about how he would break the news to Swarnima. He envisioned different scenarios, each one making him smile. He wanted the moment to be perfect. As he zipped up his suitcase, he paused for a moment, taking in the room around him. This place had been his temporary refuge, a space where he had grappled with his emotions and made a significant decision about his future. It was a bittersweet feeling, knowing he was leaving behind a chapter of uncertainty for one filled with hope and new beginnings. Yajat sat on the edge of his bed, his phone in hand, contemplating his journey. He opened his gallery and scrolled through the pictures of his time in Bangalore. Each image told a story of resilience and determination. Despite the challenges, he had found a way to carve out a path that felt right. He then switched to his chat with Swarnima, reading through their messages. Her words had been a constant source of comfort, and he was eager to see her reaction to his surprise. Before going to bed, Yajat sent a quick message to his family, letting them know his plans for the next day. He then set an early alarm, wanting to ensure he had enough time to get to the airport without any rush. The excitement made it difficult to sleep, but eventually, exhaustion took over, and he drifted into a light slumber, his mind filled with thoughts of Swarnima and the new journey ahead.

CHAPTER VIII

SECRETS AND SURPRISES

Yajat had spent a month in Bangalore, a city that had never quite felt like home. The bustling streets and vibrant nightlife did little to fill the void he felt inside. Despite the new experiences and people he met, there was always something missing—a sense of belonging, a connection that felt right. Now, back in Delhi, he could hardly contain his excitement. The prospect of surprising Swarnima filled him with a joy he hadn't felt in a long time. Staying with his friend Aditya was a temporary solution, but it gave Yajat the stability he needed while he figured out his next steps. Aditya 's apartment, with its familiar clutter and comforting disarray, was a stark contrast to the impersonal hotel room he had called home in Bangalore. Here, he felt grounded, surrounded by memories and the warmth of friendship. Every morning, Yajat woke up with a renewed sense of purpose. The bustling streets of Delhi, the familiar chaos, and the comforting hum of the city reminded him why he had missed this place so much. More than anything, he was eager to see Swarnima. The thought of surprising her made his heart race with anticipation. Yajat's mind buzzed with ideas on how to surprise her. Should he show up at her favorite coffee shop? Or maybe wait outside her hostel? He knew that whatever he chose, it had to be special—something that would convey how much he had missed her and how important she had become in his life.

One evening, as he sat on Aditya's balcony, sipping his coffee and watching the city lights flicker to life, an idea struck him. He remembered how Swarnima had once mentioned her love for sunsets. She had said they made her feel peaceful, a perfect end to even the most chaotic day. What if he could recreate that moment for her? The next morning, Yajat set his plan into motion. He spent hours arranging everything, ensuring that the surprise would be perfect. He chose a spot on the terrace of his favourite café, Rahul's cafe, one that offered a breathtaking view of the city skyline. As the day wore on, he felt a mixture of excitement and nervousness. He couldn't wait to see the look on Swarnima's face when she realized he was back.

When everything was ready, he sent her a message, keeping it vague to maintain the element of surprise. "Could you go Rahul's at 5pm? I have something there for you!"

After sending the message to Swarnima, Yajat decided to pay a visit to Rahul's café. It had been a month since he last saw his friend, and he knew that

Rahul would be equally surprised and delighted to see him. As he approached the café, the familiar aroma of freshly brewed coffee and baked goods wafted through the air, bringing a smile to his face.

Pushing open the door, Yajat was greeted by the comforting ambiance of the place that had been his second home. Rahul was behind the counter, busy preparing a latte, his back turned to the entrance. Yajat walked in quietly, leaning against the counter with a smirk on his face.

"Hey, Rahul! Got room for one more regular?" he called out, his voice filled with playful excitement.

Rahul turned around, and his eyes widened in shock. "Yajat! What are you doing here?" he exclaimed, nearly dropping the milk frother in his hand.

Yajat laughed, stepping forward to give Rahul a warm hug. "I'm back, my friend. Bangalore just wasn't the same without this place," he said, patting Rahul on the back.

Rahul pulled back, still looking at Yajat with a mixture of surprise and happiness. "I can't believe you're here! When did you get back?"

"Just today. I wanted to surprise everyone, especially you," Yajat replied, grinning.

Rahul shook his head in disbelief. "This is amazing! You have no idea how much we've missed you here. The place just hasn't been the same without your evening visits."

Yajat chuckled, feeling a warmth spread through him. "Well, I'm here now. And I have a little plan to surprise Swarnima," he said, lowering his voice conspiratorially.

Rahul raised an eyebrow, intrigued. "Oh? Do tell."

Yajat leaned in, explaining his idea to surprise

Swarnima at the café with the sunset view. "She loves sunsets, and I thought it would be the perfect way to show her how much I missed her. I've arranged everything for this evening."

Rahul's face lit up with approval. "That's a brilliant idea, Yajat. She's going to love it. I'm glad you're finally opening up to her. She's been so persistent, trying to get through to you."

Yajat nodded, a sense of determination filling him. "I know. And I'm grateful for her persistence. It's time I stop letting my past hold me back."

Rahul clapped him on the shoulder. "That's the spirit. Now, go make that surprise perfect. I'll handle things here."

With a grateful smile, Yajat thanked Rahul and made his way back to the café where he would meet Swarnima. The excitement and anticipation of the reunion filled him with hope. He was ready to embrace this new chapter, leaving behind the shadows of his past.

As the sun began to dip towards the horizon, casting a golden hue over the city, Yajat positioned himself in the café with the perfect view of the sunset. His heart raced with anticipation. He had coordinated with Rahul to ensure that Swarnima would arrive at the café under the pretense of a casual meet-up. The table was set beautifully with her favorite flowers and a couple of her preferred snacks, all illuminated by the soft glow of candlelight. The door to the café opened, and Yajat's heart skipped a beat. Swarnima walked in, her eyes scanning the room until they landed on Yajat. Her expression morphed from confusion to surprise, and finally to sheer joy. She hurried towards him, her eyes glistening with emotion.

"Yajat! What…how…?" Swarnima's voice trailed off as she reached him.

Yajat stood up, a broad smile on his face, and opened his arms wide. Swarnima didn't hesitate. She rushed into his embrace, and they held each other tightly, like lost lovers reunited after a long separation. The world around them seemed to blur, leaving just the two of them in that moment of blissful reunion.

"I can't believe you're here," Swarnima whispered, pulling back slightly to look into Yajat's eyes, her own brimming with tears of happiness.

"I'm here," Yajat said softly, brushing a strand of hair from her face. "And I'm back for good."

Swarnima's eyes widened in astonishment. "You mean…?"

"Yes," Yajat confirmed with a nod, his smile widening. "I'm not going back to Bangalore. I've decided to stay here. I realized this is where I belong, where I'm happiest."

Swarnima's face lit up with a radiant smile. "This is like a dream, Yajat! I'm so happy you're back."

Yajat chuckled, his heart swelling with joy at her reaction. "And there's more. I'm planning to move into a flat here. Something more permanent than my friend's place."

Swarnima clapped her hands in delight. "That's amazing! I'm so glad you're staying. This feels like a fairy tale."

They sat down at the beautifully arranged table, the sunset casting a warm glow over them. The atmosphere was filled with an undeniable sense of contentment and excitement. They chatted animatedly, catching up on everything they had missed in each other's lives.

Swarnima's laughter rang through the café, blending with the soft background music. "I can't believe you kept this a secret," she teased, her eyes sparkling with delight.

Yajat grinned. "I wanted to surprise you properly. And I'm glad it worked."

They talked about Yajat's plans for the flat, with Swarnima eagerly offering suggestions for decoration and making the place feel like home. Their conversation flowed effortlessly, punctuated by shared laughter and genuine smiles. As the evening progressed, they found themselves more relaxed, basking in each other's company. It was as if all the time apart had only strengthened their bond, making their reunion even sweeter.

"This moment," Swarnima said softly, gazing at Yajat with a mix of affection and wonder, "it feels perfect. Like everything is falling into place."

Yajat nodded, reaching across the table to take her hand. "It does. And I'm grateful for it. For you."

Swarnima squeezed his hand, her smile radiant. "Here's to new beginnings."

They clinked their glasses together, sealing their reunion with a promise of a brighter future. In that cozy corner of the café, with the city's skyline bathed in the soft hues of twilight, Yajat and Swarnima embraced their new chapter, ready to face whatever life had in store for them, together.

CHAPTER IX

A HOME OF OUR OWN

Yajat had embarked on the journey of finding a new flat with a mix of excitement and trepidation. Each day after work, he would comb through listings, meticulously evaluating every detail. The task proved to be more challenging than he had anticipated. Yet, through every step of the process, Swarnima was there, offering her unwavering support and keen eye for detail. They spent countless evenings exploring different neighbourhoods, assessing the vibe and accessibility of each area. Yajat was particular about finding a place that felt like home, a sanctuary where he could unwind after long days at the office. Swarnima's input was invaluable; her insights into the liveability and charm of each locale helped narrow down the choices. One late afternoon, as they walked through a bustling street filled with cafes and parks, Yajat turned to Swarnima. “I think this area has potential,” he said, noting the lively yet serene atmosphere. Swarnima nodded, her eyes scanning the surroundings thoughtfully. They viewed a plethora of flats, each with its own set of pros and cons. Some were too small, others lacked the essential charm, and a few were just out of budget. Yet, they pressed on, buoyed by the shared goal of finding the perfect place for Yajat.

One day, while scrolling through yet another list of potential flats, Swarnima's eyes lit up. “Look at this one,” she exclaimed, showing Yajat the screen. The flat was located on the 20th floor of a modern high-rise, boasting a spacious balcony with a breathtaking view of the city. Intrigued, they arranged a viewing for the next day. As they stepped into the flat, the first thing that struck them was the natural light flooding the space. The open-plan living area led to a large balcony, offering a panoramic view of the city skyline. The sight was nothing short of mesmerizing.

“This feels right,” Yajat murmured, taking in the view. Swarnima smiled, sensing his excitement. “It’s perfect,” she agreed. The balcony, with its expansive view, felt like a gateway to endless possibilities, a place where Yajat could reflect and find peace.

The flat had everything Yajat had been looking for: a comfortable living space, a modern kitchen, and a bedroom that exuded warmth. Swarnima's approval sealed the deal. They knew this was the place where Yajat could truly start his new chapter. The decision was made swiftly, and within a week, Yajat had secured the flat. The paperwork was finalized, and the move-in date was set for a weekend to ensure it wouldn't interfere with his office routine. Yajat felt a sense of relief and excitement wash over him. After nearly a month of searching, he had found a place he could call home. Swarnima was there every step of the way, helping him coordinate the move, selecting furnishings, and even offering to help with the actual moving process. Her presence was a constant source of comfort and encouragement, making the entire experience less daunting and more enjoyable. Standing on the balcony of his soon-to-be home, Yajat took a deep breath, savoring the cityscape that stretched out before him. He felt a profound sense of accomplishment and gratitude. The journey had been long and filled with challenges, but with Swarnima by his side, he had found the perfect place to start anew.

"This is it," he said, turning to Swarnima with a smile. "This is home."

Swarnima beamed back at him, her eyes reflecting the shared joy of their achievement. "I'm so happy for you, Yajat. This is just the beginning of something wonderful." As the weekend approached, Yajat prepared for the move, filled with anticipation for the new memories he would create in his beautiful new flat.

The day of the move arrived, bringing with it a sense of both excitement and trepidation. Yajat woke up early, his mind buzzing with anticipation. Swarnima arrived shortly after, her face lit up with enthusiasm as she greeted him. They had a full day ahead, and the numerous boxes stacked in the hallway were a testament to the task at hand. They started with the heaviest items first, carefully maneuvering furniture through the narrow hallways and into the elevator. It was a physically demanding task, but Yajat was grateful for Swarnima's help. She was a whirlwind of energy, directing the movers and making sure everything was placed exactly where it needed to be.

"How did you manage to pack so much?" Swarnima teased as she helped him lift a particularly heavy box labeled 'Books.'

Yajat chuckled, wiping the sweat from his forehead. "Years of collecting," he replied. "I guess I never realized how much I had until I had to move it all."

By midday, they had made significant progress. The furniture was in place, and the boxes were steadily being unpacked. Swarnima took charge of organizing the kitchen, meticulously arranging dishes and utensils in their new home. Yajat focused on the living room, setting up his bookshelves and placing his beloved collection of novels and memorabilia on display. As the afternoon wore on, the apartment began to take shape. Each item found its place, and the once chaotic space started to feel like a home. Yajat couldn't help but marvel at the transformation. It was more than just a physical change; it was the beginning of a new chapter in his life.

Swarnima, noticing his thoughtful expression, placed a reassuring hand on his shoulder. "It's really coming together, isn't it?" she said, her eyes sparkling with shared excitement.

Yajat nodded, feeling a wave of gratitude. "I

couldn't have done it without you, Swarnima. Thank you for everything."

They continued to work tirelessly, the hours slipping by unnoticed. With each box they emptied, the apartment became more organized, more personal. The sun was beginning its descent, casting a warm, golden glow through the windows, when they finally tackled the last box.

"That's the last of it," Swarnima said with a satisfied sigh, collapsing onto the couch.

Yajat joined her, feeling a mixture of exhaustion and elation. "I can't believe we did it," he said, his voice tinged with disbelief. "It actually feels like home."

Swarnima smiled, her eyes reflecting the same sense of accomplishment. "It is home, Yajat. Your home."

As they sat there, catching their breath, Yajat's gaze drifted toward the balcony. "Shall we?" he asked, gesturing toward the inviting view outside. Swarnima nodded, and they both rose, stepping out onto the balcony. The city sprawled out before them, bathed in the soft hues of the setting sun. It was a breathtaking sight, one that made the entire day's efforts worthwhile. They stood side by side, the cool evening breeze gently brushing against their faces. There was a comfortable silence between them, a sense of shared contentment. Yajat felt a profound sense of peace, as if all the pieces of his life were finally falling into place.

Swarnima broke the silence, her voice soft and thoughtful. "It's beautiful, isn't it? The view, the moment... everything."

Yajat turned to look at her, his heart swelling with gratitude and something more, something deeper. "It is," he agreed, his voice barely above a whisper. "Thank you for being here, Swarnima. For helping me through this."

She met his gaze, her eyes filled with warmth. "I wouldn't have missed it for the world, Yajat."

In that moment, Yajat felt a connection, a bond that went beyond friendship. The intimacy of the day, the shared laughter, and the mutual support had brought them closer. He realized that this was more than just a move; it was the start of something new and beautiful.

As the sun disappeared below the horizon, the city lights twinkling in the distance, an unspoken understanding passed between Yajat and Swarnima. The intimacy of the moment, the shared experiences of the day, and the comfort of their newfound closeness created an undeniable connection. Swarnima turned to Yajat, her eyes reflecting the myriad of emotions she felt. Yajat gently took her hand, feeling the warmth of her touch. Without a word, they moved closer, the distance between them evaporating. Yajat's heart raced as he leaned in, their lips meeting in a tender, hesitant kiss that quickly deepened, fueled by the emotions they had been quietly nurturing. They retreated into the apartment, the warmth of their embrace guiding them. The world outside faded away as they lost themselves in each other, their feelings culminating in a night of shared intimacy and unspoken promises. In the quiet aftermath, they lay intertwined, the weight of the day and the significance of their connection settling over them. Yajat knew that this was the beginning of something profound, something that would forever change the course of their lives. They drifted off to sleep, wrapped in each other's arms, ready to face whatever the future held together.

CHAPTER X

The Thrill of Togetherness

The next morning, the soft rays of dawn filtered through the curtains, casting a gentle glow over the room. Yajat woke up first, feeling the warmth of Swarnima's body nestled against his. For a moment, he just lay there, watching her sleep, her features serene and beautiful. The events of the previous night still played vividly in his mind, bringing a smile to his lips. He gently brushed a strand of hair away from her face, his touch feather-light so as not to wake her. Unable to resist, he leaned down and placed a soft kiss on her forehead. Swarnima stirred slightly, her eyes fluttering open to meet his. She smiled, a look of contentment washing over her face as she stretched.

"Good morning," Yajat whispered, his voice filled with tenderness.

"Good morning," Swarnima replied, her voice husky with sleep. "Did you sleep well?"

"Better than I have in a long time," he admitted, his eyes never leaving hers. "How about you?"

"Perfect," she said, her smile widening.

Yajat gently disentangled himself from her embrace and sat up. "Stay here. I'll make us some breakfast."

Swarnima watched him as he got out of bed and pulled on a pair of sweatpants and a t-shirt. He glanced back at her with a playful grin before heading to the kitchen. She snuggled deeper into the covers, feeling a warmth that had nothing to do with the blankets. In the kitchen, Yajat moved around with a newfound sense of purpose. He wanted to make something special for Swarnima, to show her how much she meant to him. He decided on a simple yet heartfelt breakfast: scrambled eggs, toast, and freshly brewed coffee. As he cooked, he couldn't help but reflect on how much his life had changed in such a short time. Swarnima's presence had become a beacon of light, dispelling the shadows of his past. He realized that for the first time in years, he was genuinely happy. The aroma of the coffee and sizzling eggs soon filled the apartment, prompting Swarnima to join him in the kitchen, wrapped in a blanket.

"That smells amazing," she said, leaning against the doorway and watching him with a fond smile.

"I hope it tastes as good as it smells," Yajat replied, plating the food and setting it on the small dining table. He poured them each a cup of coffee and gestured for her to sit.

They ate together, talking and laughing about everything and nothing. It was a simple, ordinary moment, but it felt extraordinary to both of them. As they finished their meal, Swarnima looked around the apartment and then back at Yajat.

"You know," she began, "I've been thinking. I really enjoy spending time here with you. It feels like home."

Yajat reached across the table and took her hand in his. "I've been thinking the same thing. You're always welcome here, Swarnima. You don't have to ask."

Days turned into weeks, and Swarnima's presence in Yajat's apartment became more frequent. She started leaving a few essentials at his place: a toothbrush, some clothes, her favorite books. Yajat loved having her around. Her laughter filled the rooms, and her touch brought warmth and comfort. They fell into a routine that felt natural and unforced. In the mornings, they would wake up together, often with Yajat making breakfast and Swarnima brewing coffee. They spent their evenings curled up on the couch, watching movies, talking about their days, or simply enjoying each other's company. The transition was seamless, and before they knew it, they had slipped into a comfortable rhythm that felt very much like living together. One evening, as they sat on the balcony watching the city lights twinkle below, Swarnima rested her head on Yajat's shoulder. "Do you realize how much time we've been spending together?" she asked softly.

"I do," Yajat replied, wrapping his arm around her. "And I wouldn't have it any other way."

"It's like we've accidentally moved in together," she said with a light laugh.

Yajat chuckled, his heart swelling with affection. "I think it's the best accident that could have happened."

They shared a tender kiss, both of them aware of how their lives had intertwined so effortlessly. It was a relationship built on mutual respect, trust, and a deep connection that had grown stronger with each passing day. Swarnima's things gradually filled the apartment. Her clothes hung next to Yajat's in the closet, her toiletries took up space in the bathroom, and her books found a home on his shelves. It wasn't an official move-in, but it felt just as significant. Their days were filled with the simple joys of living together. They cooked meals side by side, went grocery shopping, and spent lazy Sundays in bed, talking about their dreams and plans for the future. The apartment, once Yajat's solitary refuge, had become a shared space filled with love and laughter.

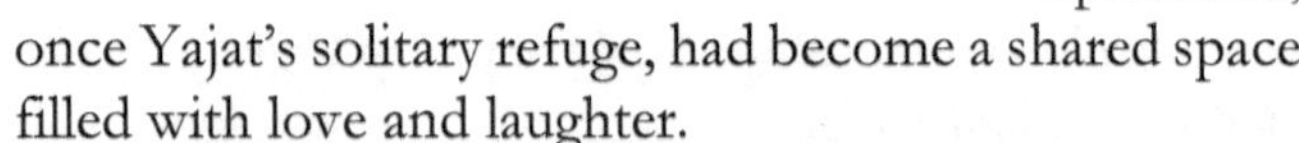

One night, as they lay in bed, Swarnima turned to Yajat and whispered, "Thank you for letting me into your life."

Yajat pulled her closer, his heart full. "Thank you for being a part of it. I can't imagine it without you."

As they drifted off to sleep, the city below them continued its ceaseless hum, but within the walls of their home, a new chapter of their lives was unfolding. They had found each other, and together, they were building something beautiful.

In the small moments of their everyday lives, Yajat and Swarnima found countless opportunities to express their love and support for each other. Whether it was sharing a meal, cuddling on the couch, or simply holding hands as they walked through the city streets, their bond only grew stronger with each passing day. Yajat would often surprise Swarnima with little gestures of affection, like leaving notes for her to find or bringing home her favorite flowers just because. Swarnima, in turn, would cook his favorite meals or offer a comforting hug when he needed it most. Their evenings together became sacred rituals, a time when they could unwind from the stresses of the day and simply enjoy each other's company. They would talk for hours about anything and everything, their conversations ranging from light-hearted banter to deeper, more meaningful topics. As the days turned into weeks and the weeks into months, Yajat and Swarnima found themselves longing for each other's presence more and more. They would count down the hours until they could be together again, eagerly anticipating the moment when they could wrap each other in a tight embrace and forget about the outside world for a while. Their unofficial live-in arrangement brought them closer than ever before. They shared their hopes and dreams, their fears and insecurities, knowing that they had each other's unwavering support no matter what. They celebrated each other's successes and comforted each other in times of failure, always standing by each other's side through thick and thin. In the quiet moments before bed, they would lie in each other's arms, their hearts beating in sync as they drifted off to sleep. And as they slept, their dreams were filled with visions of a future together, a future where their love would only continue to grow stronger with each passing day. Their love was not defined by grand gestures or extravagant displays of affection, but by the simple, everyday moments they shared together. In each other's arms, they found solace, strength, and above all, a deep and abiding love that would carry them through whatever challenges life threw their way.

CHAPTER XI

Heartfelt Moments

Yajat sat on the balcony, gazing out at the city skyline as the sun dipped below the horizon, casting a golden glow over the buildings. The past year had been a whirlwind, and as he took a deep breath, he couldn't help but reflect on how much his life had changed. His notions of love, boundaries, and everything in between had evolved in ways he had never anticipated. A year ago, Yajat was a man encased in emotional armour, shielding himself from the world and anyone who might try to get too close. His past experiences had left him wary, hesitant to trust, and reluctant to open his heart again. Love, to him, was a concept fraught with pain and disappointment. But then Swarnima had entered his life, and everything began to change. Swarnima had been a beacon of light in his otherwise guarded existence. Her persistence, patience, and genuine care had slowly chipped away at the walls he had built around his heart. He remembered their first meeting, the awkwardness, and his initial reluctance to engage. Yet, despite his resistance, she had remained, offering friendship, and understanding without expecting anything in return.

As their relationship blossomed, Yajat found himself confronting his fears and insecurities. Swarnima had a way of seeing through his facade, recognizing the vulnerability he tried so hard to conceal. She never pushed too hard but always encouraged him to be his authentic self. In doing so, she helped him realize that love didn't have to be a source of pain. It could be a source of strength and comfort, a safe haven where he could truly be himself. Over the months, Yajat had experienced a profound shift in his perceptions. He had always been wary of dependence, viewing it as a weakness. But with Swarnima, he discovered that interdependence could be beautiful. It wasn't about losing oneself in another person; it was about finding balance, where both individuals supported and uplifted each other. His notions of boundaries had also transformed. Previously, he had kept people at arm's length, afraid that letting them in would mean losing control. But Swarnima had shown him that healthy boundaries weren't about keeping people out; they were about creating space where both partners felt respected and valued. She had taught him the importance of communication and compromise, and in doing so, she had helped him build a relationship founded on mutual respect and understanding.

Yajat had also undergone significant personal

growth. Swarnima's unwavering belief in him had bolstered his confidence. She had encouraged him to pursue his passions, and with her support, he had taken on new challenges and explored new opportunities. Her belief in his potential had inspired him to believe in himself, and as a result, he had achieved things he never thought possible. Reflecting on the past year, Yajat realized how much he had changed. He had gone from a man afraid of love to someone who embraced it fully. He had learned that love wasn't about grand gestures or perfect moments; it was about the small, everyday acts of care and consideration. It was about being there for each other through the highs and lows, celebrating victories, and providing comfort during defeats. He had also come to understand the importance of vulnerability. In opening up to Swarnima, he had found a sense of freedom and release. He no longer felt the need to hide behind a mask or pretend to be someone he wasn't. With her, he could be raw and real, knowing that she would accept him just as he was. Yajat's life had taken a turn he had never expected, and as he sat on the balcony, he felt a deep sense of gratitude. The journey had been challenging, filled with moments of doubt and fear, but it had also been incredibly rewarding. He had discovered a new capacity for love and connection, and in doing so, he had found a happiness he hadn't known was possible. As he looked out at the city, Yajat knew that the future would hold its own set of challenges, but he felt ready to face them. With Swarnima by his side, he had the strength and resilience to take on whatever came their way. His life had changed profoundly, and he couldn't wait to see what the next chapter would bring.

Swarnima had been under the weather for a few days, but one morning, she woke up with a fever that wouldn't break. Yajat immediately sensed the severity of her condition and took swift action. He called in sick at work, determined to stay home and take care of her. He couldn't bear the thought of leaving her alone when she needed him the most. As the fever raged, Swarnima lay in bed, shivering and weak. Yajat stayed by her side, keeping a constant watch over her. He prepared a warm bowl of soup and gently fed her, encouraging her to eat despite her lack of appetite. He massaged her temples when her headaches were too much to bear and held her hand through the worst of the chills and sweats. The nights were the hardest. Swarnima would wake up multiple times, disoriented and uncomfortable. Each time, Yajat was there, ready with a cold compress or a soothing word. He barely slept, choosing instead to sit by her bed, monitoring her condition and ensuring she was as comfortable as possible. He whispered reassurances and stroked her hair, his heart aching to see her in such pain. Despite her illness, Swarnima appreciated every bit of Yajat's care. She could see the worry etched on his face and the tiredness in his eyes. One afternoon, when she felt a little better, she insisted he take a nap. "You need rest too," she said, her voice weak but determined. Yajat reluctantly agreed, lying down next to her. As he drifted off to sleep, Swarnima reached out and held his hand, grateful for his unwavering support.

When Yajat woke up, he found Swarnima trying to sit up, looking around the room. "What do you need, Swarnima?" he asked, immediately alert.

"I'm just looking for some water," she replied softly.

Yajat quickly got up and fetched a glass of water. As

he handed it to her, he noticed the small smile on her lips. "Thank you," she whispered, sipping the water slowly.

Days passed, and Swarnima's condition gradually improved. Yajat's dedication never wavered. He continued to cook for her, making sure she had nutritious meals to regain her strength. He even read to her, picking up her favorite books and bringing their characters to life with his voice. His presence was a constant comfort, and Swarnima felt herself recovering faster with him by her side.

Swarnima wasn't one to remain passive in their relationship either. Once she was back on her feet, she insisted on taking care of Yajat in return. She knew he had neglected his own needs while taking care of her, and she wanted to show her gratitude in every way possible.

One evening, as Yajat returned home from work, he found Swarnima busy in the kitchen. The aroma of his favorite dish filled the air. "You should be resting," he said, a mixture of concern and admiration in his voice.

"I'm feeling much better," Swarnima replied with a smile. "And you deserve a nice meal after everything you've done for me."

Yajat sat down at the table, watching her move around with ease. He felt a warm sensation of happiness and love fill his heart. They shared a quiet dinner, enjoying each other's company and the simple pleasure of being together.

Swarnima went beyond cooking. She insisted on washing his clothes, despite his protests. "It's the least I can do," she argued, not taking no for an answer. Yajat couldn't help but smile at her determination. He appreciated her gestures, knowing they came from a place of genuine care and love.

Their bond deepened through these acts of care and concern. They learned to lean on each other, finding strength in their partnership. The love they shared was evident in every small gesture, every kind word, and every moment of support.

As they sat together one evening, watching the sunset from their balcony, Yajat took Swarnima's hand in his. "Thank you for being here," he said softly.

Swarnima squeezed his hand and leaned her head on his shoulder. "Thank you for everything, Yajat. I couldn't have asked for a better partner."

In that moment, they both knew that their love was built on more than just romance. It was built on mutual respect, unwavering support, and a deep understanding of each other's needs. They were a team, ready to face whatever challenges life might throw their way, together.

CHAPTER XII

Ripples In The Ocean

Not everything is always good, and that was the case with Yajat and Swarnima. Their relationship, like any other, had its ups and downs. Yajat was trying to overcome his past mistakes and move forward, but the pressures of life and work often created tension between them. They both cared deeply for each other, but sometimes the stress of their individual lives spilled over into their relationship. Yajat was finding it hard to balance the demands of his job with his personal life. The constant pressure to perform at work left him exhausted and irritable. Swarnima, on the other hand, was dealing with her own challenges. As an explorer, her passion often took her on outings and explorations, leaving Yajat feeling lonely. These feelings would sometimes manifest as frustration, leading to arguments that neither of them truly wanted.

One evening, after a particularly gruelling day at work, Yajat came home to find Swarnima packing for another trip. The sight of her suitcase pushed him over the edge. "You're leaving again?" he asked, his voice tinged with irritation.

Swarnima looked up, sensing the tension in his voice. "It's just for a few days, Yajat. I told you about this last week."

"I know, but it feels like you're always gone," he replied, struggling to keep his emotions in check. "I barely get to see you."

Swarnima sighed, feeling the familiar sting of frustration. "I have my life too, Yajat. It's important to me."

"I understand that," he said, his tone softening slightly. "But sometimes it feels like it is more important than us."

They stood in silence for a moment, both grappling with their feelings. Swarnima approached him, placing a hand on his arm. "Yajat, I love you. But I also love what I do."

Yajat nodded, realizing that his frustration was more about his own struggles than anything Swarnima was doing. "I'm sorry. It's just been a tough day."

Swarnima smiled, a hint of relief in her eyes. "I know. Let's talk about it."

They sat down and discussed their feelings, airing out their frustrations and concerns. It wasn't always easy, but these conversations helped them understand each other better. They realized that their arguments often stemmed from external pressures rather than any real issue between them. One weekend, after a particularly tense week, Swarnima decided to surprise

Yajat with a special dinner. She cooked his favorite meal and set the table with candles and flowers. When Yajat came home, he was greeted by the warm, inviting scene. His stress melted away as he realized how much effort Swarnima had put into making him feel appreciated.

"What's all this?" he asked, a smile spreading across his face.

"Just a little something to show you how much I care," she replied, wrapping her arms around him.

Yajat hugged her tightly, feeling the tension of the week dissipate. "Thank you, Swarnima. I really needed this."

They enjoyed the meal together, talking and laughing as they rekindled their connection. These moments of reconciliation reminded them why they were together and how much they meant to each other. Another time, it was Yajat who took the initiative. He noticed that Swarnima was feeling down after a difficult project. To cheer her up, he planned a weekend getaway to a nearby hill station. When he revealed the surprise, Swarnima's eyes lit up with joy.

"You're amazing, Yajat," she said, hugging him tightly. "I can't believe you did this for me."

"I just want us to be happy," he replied, holding her close.

The trip was exactly what they needed. They spent the weekend hiking, talking, and simply enjoying each other's company. It was a reminder that, despite the challenges, their love was strong enough to weather any storm. Though they had their share of arguments and frustrations, Yajat and Swarnima always found a way to reconcile. Their commitment to each other and their willingness to communicate kept their relationship strong. They learned to navigate the rough patches, knowing that their love was worth the effort.

One sunny weekend, Yajat and Swarnima were enjoying a lazy afternoon together. They lounged on the couch, sharing stories and laughter, revelling in each other's company. In a playful mood, Yajat dared Swarnima to exchange phones for a few minutes.

"Come on, it'll be fun!" he said, grinning mischievously.

Swarnima raised an eyebrow, her eyes sparkling with amusement. "You sure you want to see all the embarrassing selfies and random notes I have?"

"Absolutely," Yajat chuckled. "I bet I have more embarrassing stuff on mine."

They both laughed, the idea seeming innocent and light-hearted. Swarnima handed over her phone with a smirk, but as Yajat took it, she suddenly hesitated.

"Actually, wait," she said, reaching to take it back.

Yajat, thinking she was still playing, held it away from her. "Oh no, you can't back out now!"

Swarnima's expression changed. "Yajat, seriously, give it back."

Confused, Yajat frowned. "What's the big deal, Swarnima? It's just a game."

"It's not just a game," she replied, her tone sharp. "It's my privacy."

Yajat's playful mood faded, replaced by a mix of confusion and frustration. "Privacy? But we trust each other, don't we? What are you hiding?"

Swarnima's eyes flashed with anger. "It's not about hiding anything, Yajat. It's about respecting boundaries."

He didn't back down. "Boundaries? We're together since the past year, Swarnima. We should be able to share everything."

"Sharing everything doesn't mean giving up my right to privacy," she snapped, grabbing for her phone.

Yajat pulled it back once more, more out of stubbornness than anything else. "Why are you being so defensive?"

Swarnima stood up, her face flushed with anger. "Because you're not listening to me! It's not about you, it's about my principles."

Their playful afternoon had taken a serious turn, and Yajat's persistence had pushed Swarnima to her limit. She felt invaded, her personal space disrespected. Yajat, on the other hand, felt hurt and confused by her resistance, interpreting it as a lack of trust.

"Fine," he said, tossing her phone onto the couch. "If you don't trust me, maybe there's a reason for it."

Swarnima picked up her phone, her hands shaking with anger and hurt. "You're unbelievable, Yajat. This isn't about trust. It's about respecting each other's boundaries."

"Boundaries?" he repeated, incredulous. "We're supposed to be a team, Swarnima. Teams don't have boundaries."

"They do when it comes to personal privacy!" she retorted, her voice rising. "You can't just bulldoze through my boundaries because you feel insecure."

The room was thick with tension, both of them glaring at each other, breaths heavy. It was a clash of ideals, both feeling misunderstood and hurt. The silence that followed was suffocating.

After a long, agonizing moment, Yajat sighed deeply. "Swarnima, I'm sorry. I didn't mean to invade your privacy. I just... I just thought it was a harmless game."

Swarnima's shoulders dropped, the anger in her eyes softening. "I know, Yajat. But you have to understand that some things are personal. It doesn't mean I don't trust you. It's just... mine."

He nodded slowly, stepping closer to her. "I get it now. I'm sorry I pushed you."

Swarnima sighed, tears brimming in her eyes. "I'm sorry too, for snapping at you. It just felt like you didn't respect my boundaries."

Yajat took her hands in his, pulling her into a gentle embrace. "I promise to be more respectful of your privacy. Can we move past this?"

She nodded against his chest. "Yes, we can. Thank you for understanding."

They held each other for a long time, letting the warmth of their embrace dissolve the tension. It was a small event, but it taught them both a valuable lesson about respect and boundaries. Their maturity in resolving the conflict only strengthened their bond, proving once again that their love could withstand any challenge.

CHAPTER XIII

Brewing Storms

More time had elapsed since Yajat and Swarnima first embarked on their journey of living together. In the beginning, their relationship had been a harmonious blend of mutual respect and understanding. But as months passed, subtle cracks began to appear, born out of their differing ideologies and approaches to life. They were both mature individuals, always striving to reconcile their differences, but the constant strain was beginning to take its toll.

One of the main sources of tension was their differing views on work-life balance. Yajat, a research analyst with a meticulous nature, believed in a disciplined approach to work. He often brought his work home, spending long hours in front of his laptop even on weekends. Swarnima, on the other hand, was an explorer at heart. She valued spontaneity and believed that life should be lived in the moment. Her student days allowed her to maintain a flexible schedule, and she often suggested impromptu outings.

One Saturday morning, Swarnima bounced into the living room with a bright smile. "Yajat, let's go on for a coffee today! There's this beautiful place not far from here, I've been wanting to explore."

Yajat looked up from his laptop, his brow furrowing slightly. "I can't, Swarnima. I have to finish this report. Maybe some other time?"

Her face fell, but she quickly masked her disappointment. "You always say that, Yajat. It's like you never have time for anything else."

He sighed, closing his laptop and rubbing his temples. "It's not that I don't want to spend time with you. It's just that I have responsibilities, deadlines. You know that."

She nodded, her frustration barely contained. "I do know that, but it feels like you're always choosing work over us."

Another area of conflict was their differing financial philosophies. Yajat was a saver, cautious and conservative with his money. Swarnima, however, believed in enjoying and was more inclined to spend on experiences and things that brought immediate joy.

One evening, Swarnima excitedly showed Yajat a new camera she had bought. "Look at this, Yajat! Isn't it amazing? It's perfect for me to capture the moments of my explorations."

Yajat forced a smile, though his concern was evident. "It's great, Swarnima. But was it really necessary? We should save for the future, not just spend on whims."

Her eyes flashed with irritation. "It's not a whim, Yajat. I see it as an investment for myself, to make myself better. And besides, we can't just keep saving and never enjoy our lives."

He took a deep breath, trying to keep his voice calm. "I understand that, but we need to be more careful. We can't just spend without thinking about the long-term."

Their disagreements extended beyond just work and finances. Even their household routines became a point of contention. Yajat liked structure and order, while Swarnima thrived in chaos and spontaneity. One night, after a particularly long day at work, Yajat came home to find the living room in disarray. Books and papers were scattered everywhere, remnants of Swarnima's creative process.

"Swarnima," he called out, frustration lacing his tone. "Can we please keep the place tidy? I can't relax when it's like this."

She appeared from the kitchen, wiping her hands on a towel. "I was just working on some ideas. I'll clean it up later."

He sighed, shaking his head. "It's always 'later'. I just want to come home to a clean space."

She frowned, crossing her arms. "I know, Yajat I have been trying to do it. I shouldn't have to feel like I'm walking on eggshells."

Despite these growing tensions, Yajat and Swarnima always made an effort to reconcile. They valued their relationship too much to let it be consumed by conflict. After every disagreement, they would sit down and talk it out, trying to understand each other's perspectives. One evening, after a particularly heated argument about their differing social habits—Yajat preferred quiet nights in while Swarnima enjoyed going out with friends—they sat down on the couch, exhaustion etched on their faces.

"I'm sorry, Swarnima," Yajat said, taking her hand. "I didn't mean to make you feel like your needs don't matter. I just... I get so caught up in my own way of doing things."

She squeezed his hand, her eyes softening. "I'm sorry too, Yajat. I need to remember that we're different people, and that's okay. We need to find a balance."

They spent the rest of the evening talking, not just about their differences but about their hopes and dreams. They reaffirmed their commitment to each other, vowing to work through their issues together.

As the weeks went by, their efforts to reconcile became more frequent. The underlying tensions were like a slow-burning fuse, always threatening to ignite but never quite reaching the point of explosion. Each reconciliation brought them closer, but the unresolved issues continued to linger, like shadows in the corners of their relationship.

One morning, as Yajat was preparing to leave for work, Swarnima approached him with a concerned expression. "Yajat, we need to talk."

He paused, sensing the seriousness in her tone. "What is it, Swarnima?"

She took a deep breath, looking into his eyes. "I feel like we're drifting apart. We keep having these disagreements, and it's wearing us down. We need to find a way to really address these issues, not just patch things up temporarily."

Yajat nodded slowly, his heart heavy. "You're right. We can't keep sweeping things under the rug. Let's take some time this weekend to really talk, to figure out how we can make this work better for both of us."

Swarnima smiled, relief evident in her eyes. "I'd like that, Yajat. I love you, and I want us to be happy together."

"I love you too, Swarnima," he said, pulling her into a warm embrace. "We'll get through this. Together."

Their journey was far from perfect, and the road ahead was still uncertain. But Yajat and Swarnima were determined to navigate it hand in hand, facing their challenges with the same maturity and love that had brought them together in the first place. As the days turned into weeks, the atmosphere between Yajat and Swarnima continued to oscillate between moments of tenderness and periods of mounting tension. Their efforts to reconcile after each disagreement were genuine, but the unresolved issues seemed to be accumulating like storm clouds on the horizon. The buildup of unspoken frustrations and unresolved conflicts was leading them towards a pivotal moment in their relationship. With a heavy heart, Yajat knew that the coming days would test their bond like never before. And yet, he held onto a glimmer of hope that, together, they could weather the storm and emerge stronger on the other side.

CHAPTER XIV

THE BREAKING STORM

The oscillation between peace and fights had been happening for the past two months, creating a growing tension between Yajat and Swarnima. Despite their best efforts to reconcile after each disagreement, the pent-up frustrations were becoming more challenging to ignore. They both felt the strain, trying to keep up appearances and maintain their bond, but the underlying issues were slipping out of their control. One evening, the tension reached its breaking point. It was a quiet night, and they had decided to watch a movie together. The film had started around midnight, and by 2 AM, Yajat was engrossed in the storyline, fully absorbed by the characters and the plot twists. Swarnima, however, was less focused. Her phone buzzed incessantly, drawing her attention away from the screen. At first, Yajat tried to ignore it, believing that it would eventually stop. But the constant buzzing and the glow of the screen in the darkened room became increasingly irritating. Every few minutes, Swarnima would glance at her phone, her fingers flying over the screen as she replied to messages. She seemed distracted, her mind elsewhere, and Yajat could feel his patience wearing thin. He did not want to peep over her shoulder or pry into her conversations, but the repeated disturbances were grating on his nerves. The constant notifications interrupted the flow of the movie, and Yajat could sense the growing distance between them in those moments. He felt a rising irritation, unable to fully enjoy the film with the persistent interruptions.

Finally, unable to contain his frustration any longer, Yajat paused the movie and turned to Swarnima. "Swarnima, can you please put your phone down? We're supposed to be watching this together."

Swarnima looked up, startled by his tone. "I'm just checking a few messages, Yajat. It's not a big deal."

"It is a big deal," Yajat replied, his voice edged with irritation. "We've been waiting to watch this movie together, and you're barely paying attention."

Swarnima sighed, setting her phone down for a moment. "I am paying attention, Yajat. Just because I'm checking my phone doesn't mean I'm not interested."

Yajat shook his head, his frustration bubbling over. "It feels like you're not here with me, like you're more interested in whatever's on your phone than spending time together."

Swarnima's expression hardened, the playful mood dissipating. "Why do you always have to make a big deal out of everything? It's just a phone, Yajat."

The tension that had been building for weeks finally erupted. Both of them had been trying to keep things under control, but the unresolved issues and frustrations boiled over in that moment. As the argument escalated, they both realized that this fight was about more than just a phone or a movie—it was about the deeper issues that had been simmering beneath the surface for too long.

What started as a small disagreement quickly spiraled out of control, fueled by the pent-up frustrations that had been accumulating for months. Their initial argument about the phone and the movie was merely a spark that ignited a much larger fire.

"Why do you always have to be so serious about everything?" Swarnima snapped, her voice rising in anger. "It's just a movie. It's not like we're solving world problems here."

Yajat's frustration flared. "It's not about the movie,

Swarnima. It's about being present, about spending quality time together. Lately, it feels like you're always distracted, always somewhere else."

"That's not fair," Swarnima shot back. "I make time for us, but I have other things going on too. You can't expect me to drop everything just because we're watching a movie."

Yajat's jaw tightened. "It's not just about the movie. It's about everything. When we're together, you're always on your phone. We barely talk like we used to."

Swarnima's eyes flashed with defiance. "Oh, so now it's my fault that we don't talk? Maybe if you weren't so obsessed with your work all the time, I'd feel more connected to you."

Yajat felt a surge of anger. "That's not fair, Swarnima. I work hard because I want to build a future. You know that."

"And what about our present, Yajat?" Swarnima retorted. "What's the point of building a future if our present is falling apart?"

They both paused, breathing heavily, the room filled with a tense silence. It seemed for a moment that things might calm down, that they might find a way to defuse the situation. But then, Swarnima's phone rang, breaking the fragile peace.

It was 4 AM, and the shrill ring cut through the silence like a knife. Swarnima's eyes widened in disbelief as she glanced at the caller ID. Yajat, already on edge, felt his heart drop. "Who is it?" he demanded, his voice low and intense.

Swarnima hesitated, then answered, "It's Aakash... the one we've talked about before."

Yajat's face darkened. They had discussed Aakash multiple times, and Yajat had expressed his discomfort that he has seen Aakash and knows what he thinks about her, he had even warned Swarnima about him. The fact that he was calling at such an ungodly hour only added fuel to the fire. "Why is he calling you at this time?" Yajat asked, struggling to keep his voice steady.

Swarnima looked as surprised as he was. "I don't know, Yajat. I wasn't expecting this either."

Yajat felt a surge of betrayal. "This is exactly what I'm talking about, Swarnima. Why is he calling you now?"

Swarnima's eyes filled with frustration. "I don't control when people call me, Yajat. We have talked about him and I am keeping my distance with him."

"Distance?" Yajat echoed, his voice laced with sarcasm. "One doesn't call at 4 AM unless it's an emergency. What's going on, Swarnima?"

Swarnima's patience snapped. "Nothing is going on, Yajat! You're being ridiculous. This is exactly why I don't share everything with you. You always overreact."

Yajat felt his anger boiling over. "I'm overreacting? You're the one who can't seem trust me and understand my care. How am I supposed to feel secure in this relationship if you keep secrets?"

Swarnima's face flushed with anger. "I'm not keeping secrets, Yajat. You're the one who can't trust me. This is your issue, not mine."

The argument escalated, their voices rising as they hurled accusations and defenses back and forth. The call at 4 AM had unleashed all their buried insecurities and unresolved issues, turning a simple disagreement into a full-blown fight.

Both of them overreacted, each clinging to their

perspective as if it were the only truth. Yajat, in his protective instinct, wanted Swarnima to steer clear of Aakash, whom he perceived as not being a good influence. He was acting out of care and concern, hoping to shield Swarnima from potential harm. On the other hand, Swarnima wasn't entirely wrong either. She had been maintaining a healthy distance from Aakash, but the oddity of the late-night call and the tense situation only served to ignite the conflict further. Neither of them was ready to back down. The room felt charged with unresolved emotions, the tension palpable in the air. They both stood there, their hearts pounding, their minds racing. Swarnima's face was flushed with anger and confusion, while Yajat's eyes were clouded with frustration and a hint of betrayal.

"Yajat, you're being unreasonable," Swarnima said, her voice trembling. "I've done nothing wrong. He's just a friend."

Yajat clenched his fists, trying to contain the storm of emotions swirling inside him. "Just a friend? At 4 AM? This isn't normal, Swarnima. I'm trying to protect you, to protect us."

Swarnima's eyes flashed with indignation. "Protect me? From what, Yajat? From my friends? You're not my keeper. I have my boundaries, and I've respected them."

Yajat's frustration reached a boiling point. "It's not about control, Swarnima. It's about trust and respect. I need to feel secure in this relationship, and this isn't helping."

Swarnima crossed her arms, her stance defensive. "And what about my need for trust, Yajat? You don't trust me. You're letting your past dictate our present."

The mention of his past stung. Yajat felt a rush of

anger and pain, old wounds reopening. "You don't understand, Swarnima. I've been through this before. I can't go through it again."

Swarnima's expression softened slightly, but she didn't relent. "I'm not your past, Yajat. I'm here, now. You need to let go of your ghosts and see me for who I am."

The words hung in the air, heavy with meaning. They stood there, staring at each other, their breaths coming in ragged gasps. Neither was willing to give in, their pride and pain too great. Finally, Yajat turned away, unable to bear the tension any longer. "I need some air," he muttered, walking out to the balcony. The cool morning breeze hit him, offering a momentary relief from the suffocating atmosphere inside. He leaned on the railing, staring out at the city as it slowly awoke, bathed in the soft glow of dawn. Swarnima remained inside, her mind reeling from the intensity of their argument. She sank onto the couch, burying her face in her hands. Tears welled up, but she blinked them away, refusing to give in to the sorrow that threatened to overwhelm her. Yajat stood on the balcony, his thoughts a chaotic swirl. He was frustrated with himself, with Swarnima, with the situation. The ghosts of his past relationships haunted him, making him doubt, making him fear. He had thought he was over it, but tonight had shown him just how deeply those scars ran. Swarnima, sitting alone, felt a similar turmoil. She understood Yajat's fears but couldn't help feeling hurt by his lack of trust. She had always been open and honest, yet she felt judged and scrutinized. It wasn't fair, and it wasn't what she had signed up for. Minutes turned into hours, and the first rays of the sun began to filter through the curtains. The night's cold reality was slowly giving way to the warmth of day, but the rift between them remained. They were two people who cared deeply for each other but were caught in the crossfire of misunderstandings and unresolved issues. As the sun climbed higher, they both knew they needed to talk, to resolve this. But for now, they remained apart, each lost in their thoughts, contemplating the fragility of love and trust.

CHAPTER XV

REACHING TO THE OTHER SIDE

The tension lingered in the air, heavy and suffocating, as the minutes stretched into hours. The silence between Yajat and Swarnima was deafening, each lost in their own tumultuous thoughts. The morning sun now fully illuminated the room, casting long shadows that seemed to mirror the growing distance between them. Yajat, standing on the balcony, felt a storm brewing inside him. He knew he needed to break the silence, to reach out and mend what was breaking. Summoning his courage, he walked back into the room where Swarnima sat, her face a mask of conflicting emotions.

"Swarnima," he began softly, his voice trembling with the weight of unspoken words, "we need to talk. We can't let this tear us apart."

Swarnima looked up, her eyes filled with sadness and confusion. She took a deep breath, her voice barely above a whisper. "Yajat, I need time to understand things. I need a break."

The word "break" hit Yajat like a punch to the gut. His mind immediately associated it with "breakup," the painful ending he had feared. The idea of separation, even temporary, was too much for him to bear. His heart raced, panic seeping into his voice. "A break? What does that even mean, Swarnima? Are you saying we should end this?"

Swarnima shook her head, her expression earnest yet pained. "No, Yajat, it's not like that. I just need time to think, to process everything. This constant tension isn't good for either of us. I think we should stay apart for a while, give ourselves space to calm down."

Yajat struggled to grasp the concept, his mind rebelling against the idea of being apart. "But Swarnima, I don't understand. How can time apart solve anything? I can't lose you."

Swarnima reached out, taking his hand in hers, trying to convey her sincerity. "Yajat, it's not about losing each other. It's about finding a way to make this work without the constant fighting. I love you, but I need some time to figure things out. It's for the best."

Despite his resistance, Yajat saw the determination in her eyes. He knew that pushing her further would only make things worse. His heart ached, but he nodded reluctantly. "Okay, if you think that's what's best, I'll respect your decision. But please, don't be away for too long."

Swarnima gave him a sad smile, tears welling up in her eyes. She leaned in, giving him a gentle kiss on the cheek. "Thank you for understanding, Yajat. I promise, this isn't the end. We just need to heal."

With that, she gathered her things and left the apartment, leaving Yajat standing alone in the living room, feeling a profound emptiness. The door closed behind her, the sound echoing in the silent room, a painful reminder of the space that now lay between them. Yajat sank onto the couch, his mind a whirlwind of emotions. He felt lost, torn between hope and despair. The word "break" echoed in his mind, a haunting reminder of his fear of losing Swarnima forever. He knew he had to trust her, to trust that this time apart would indeed heal their wounds. But for now, all he could do was wait and hope that their love would withstand this storm.

The days of separation felt like an eternity to Yajat. Each day without Swarnima was a reminder of how deeply he missed her presence. He struggled with the emptiness that her absence created, the silence of his apartment amplifying his loneliness. The little things she did, the way she hummed while cooking, her playful banter, and even the way she would leave her books scattered around, all became painfully vivid in his memory. Yajat found himself constantly reaching for his phone, hoping for a message or a call from her. Nights were the hardest, as he lay in bed, longing for the comfort of her touch, the sound of her voice, and the warmth of her smile. He realized how much he loved her, how much he needed her in his life. As he reflected on their time together, he understood the true depth of his feelings. He didn't just love Swarnima; he wanted to spend his life with her. The separation made him realize that her presence was not just comforting but essential. He missed her habits, her quirks, and her unwavering support. In these days apart, Yajat came to a profound realization: Swarnima was his anchor, and he couldn't imagine a future without her. He was determined to reconcile and take their relationship to the next level, knowing that together, they could overcome any obstacle.

After days of turmoil and introspection, Yajat decided to reach out to Swarnima. He needed to make things right. Summoning all his courage, he called her and asked if they could meet and talk. Swarnima hesitated at first but agreed, suggesting Rahul's place as a neutral ground for their conversation. Rahul welcomed them with his usual warmth, sensing the gravity of the situation but keeping the atmosphere light. As they sat down in the cozy corner, the tension between Yajat and Swarnima was palpable. Rahul discreetly left them alone, understanding that they needed privacy to mend their broken relationship.

Yajat took a deep breath, breaking the silence.

"Swarnima, I'm really sorry for everything that happened. I've had a lot of time to think about it, and I realize how much I've let my past influence my actions. I never wanted to hurt you."

Swarnima looked at him, her eyes softening.

"I'm sorry too, Yajat. I should have communicated better. I know you were just being protective, but at that moment, it felt overwhelming. I didn't mean to push you away."

They both sighed, the weight of the misunderstanding slowly lifting.

Yajat continued, "I understand now that we had a miscommunication. I let my fears dictate my actions, and I projected my insecurities onto you. It wasn't fair."

Swarnima nodded. "And I should have been more

transparent about my feelings. I never intended to make you feel excluded or untrusted. We both need to work on our communication."

Yajat reached out, taking her hand.

"I've missed you so much, Swarnima. These days apart have made me realize how important you are to me. I want us to work on this relationship, to really understand each other's needs and grow together."

Swarnima squeezed his hand, a small smile forming on her lips. "I've missed you too, Yajat. Let's take this as a learning experience and make our relationship stronger. We need to be honest and open with each other."

They spent the next few hours talking, delving into the intricacies of their relationship. Yajat opened up about his insecurities, explaining how it had shaped his fears. Swarnima listened patiently, realizing how deeply her actions had affected him.

"I'm not perfect, and I have my baggage," Yajat admitted.

"But I want to move forward with you. I want us to build a future together, without letting the past dictate our present."

Swarnima smiled warmly. "We all have our pasts, Yajat. What matters is how we support each other and grow from our experiences. Let's make a pact to always communicate, no matter how difficult it might be."

Their conversation marked the beginning of a renewed effort to understand and support each other. They started setting aside time each day to talk about their feelings, ensuring that no miscommunication would fester. They learned to express their needs and fears openly, creating a safe space for both of them. Yajat also made an effort to be more patient and understanding, recognizing when his past insecurities were affecting his present actions. Swarnima, on her part, became more mindful of how her actions might be perceived and worked to reassure Yajat of her commitment. Together, they navigated the complexities of their relationship, celebrating the small victories and addressing the challenges head-on. They realized that their bond was worth fighting for and that with mutual respect and understanding, they could overcome any obstacle. Their efforts bore fruit as their relationship grew stronger and more resilient. The misunderstandings that once threatened to tear them apart became opportunities for growth and deeper connection. They discovered new facets of each other, learning to appreciate the unique qualities that made their relationship special. By the time they left Rahul's place, Yajat and Swarnima were more in tune with each other than ever before. They walked hand in hand, ready to face the future with a renewed sense of commitment and love. Their journey was far from over, but they were confident that together, they could navigate whatever life threw their way.

CHAPTER XVI

BONDS REFORGED

A month had passed since that fateful fight, and the air between Yajat and Swarnima had cleared considerably. The tension that once marred their interactions had dissipated, replaced by a renewed sense of understanding and commitment. Their relationship had taken a positive turn, growing stronger with each passing day. Yajat had undergone a significant transformation. The fight had been a wake-up call, forcing him to confront his past mistakes and insecurities. He realized that his overprotective nature and unresolved issues from his previous relationship were creating barriers between him and Swarnima. Determined to change, Yajat made a conscious effort to leave his past behind and focus on the present, on the relationship he wanted to build with Swarnima. Each morning, Yajat greeted Swarnima with a warm smile and a loving embrace, setting a positive tone for the day. He started his mornings early, preparing breakfast for them both, experimenting with new recipes to surprise her. Swarnima appreciated these small gestures, feeling cherished and valued. It was a stark contrast to the mornings filled with tension and misunderstandings they once had. One Saturday morning, Yajat woke up early to make Swarnima's favorite sandwiches. The aroma of freshly brewed coffee and sizzling sandwiches filled the air as he hummed a tune. Swarnima, awakened by the enticing smells, walked into the kitchen with a sleepy smile.

"Good morning, love," Yajat greeted her, placing a plate of perfectly golden sandwich in front of her.

"Good morning," she replied, her eyes sparkling with delight. "These look amazing!"

As they enjoyed breakfast together, they talked about their plans for the day. Yajat had arranged a surprise outing, knowing how much Swarnima loved exploring new places. He had planned a visit to a nearby botanical garden, a peaceful haven amidst the bustling city, followed by a picnic under the shade of a large oak tree.

Swarnima was thrilled, her excitement palpable. "This is perfect, Yajat. Thank you for planning this."

Yajat smiled, feeling a sense of fulfillment. "Anything for you, Swarnima. I just want to see you happy."

At the botanical garden, they wandered through the vibrant array of flowers, hand in hand. Yajat's eyes never left Swarnima, watching her light up with each new discovery. He reveled in her joy, feeling a deep sense of contentment. This was what he wanted – to make her happy and to share in her happiness. During the picnic, they sat close together, the gentle breeze rustling the leaves above them. They talked about their dreams, their fears, and their plans for the future. Yajat opened up about his past, his fears of repeating old mistakes, and his determination to be a better partner.

"I've learned so much from our time together, Swarnima," Yajat said, his voice earnest. "I don't want to let my past dictate our future. I want to grow with you, support you, and make you happy."

Swarnima looked at him with a mixture of love and admiration. "You've already changed so much, Yajat. I see the effort you're putting in, and it means the world to me. We're in this together, and we'll keep growing, hand in hand."

Their relationship flourished as they navigated this new phase. Yajat's changed behavior was evident in the small things – his patience, his willingness to listen, and his efforts to make Swarnima feel loved and appreciated. He was no longer the same person who had let his insecurities cloud his judgment. He had grown, learning to trust and communicate better. One evening, as they cuddled on the couch, Swarnima looked at Yajat with a thoughtful expression. "You know, I've noticed how much you've changed. It's like you're a different person, but in the best way possible."

Yajat smiled, pulling her closer. "I had to change, Swarnima. For you, for us. I don't want to lose what we have."

Swarnima's eyes softened with emotion. "You won't, Yajat. We're stronger than ever. And I love you for who you are, past and all."

Their days were filled with love and laughter, each

moment a testament to their growing bond. They spent weekends exploring new places, cooking meals together, and simply enjoying each other's company. The fights and misunderstandings seemed like a distant memory, overshadowed by the warmth and affection they now shared. Yajat's efforts to make Swarnima happy did not go unnoticed. She reciprocated his love and care, supporting him in his endeavors and being his constant source of strength. They had learned the importance of communication, trust, and mutual respect, and it reflected in their relationship. As the month drew to a close, Yajat looked back at how far they had come. He felt a deep sense of gratitude for Swarnima and the love they had built together. Their relationship was far from perfect, but it was real, grounded in understanding and commitment. Yajat knew that with Swarnima by his side, they could overcome any obstacle and build a beautiful future together. They had transformed their relationship from one marred by misunderstandings to one enriched by love and mutual respect. And as they looked forward to the future, they did so with the knowledge that they were stronger together, ready to face whatever life had in store for them.

As the months rolled by, Yajat and Swarnima's relationship continued to deepen and mature. The lessons they had learned from their past conflicts now served as the foundation for a stronger, more resilient bond. Swarnima, who had always been the more expressive of the two, found new ways to show her appreciation and commitment to Yajat. One evening, after a long day at work, Yajat returned home to find the apartment bathed in the soft glow of candlelight. Swarnima greeted him with a warm smile and a tender kiss, guiding him to the beautifully set dining table.

"What's all this?" Yajat asked, a mixture of surprise and curiosity in his voice.

Swarnima took his hand and led him to his seat. "I wanted to do something special for you," she said softly. "To show you how much I appreciate everything you do for me, for us."

Yajat's heart swelled with emotion. He sat down, feeling a profound sense of gratitude for the woman who had become his anchor. As they enjoyed the meal, Swarnima's eyes sparkled with a depth of emotion that words couldn't capture. After dinner, they moved to the couch, where Swarnima took Yajat's hands in hers. "Yajat, I know we've been through a lot. There have been times when things seemed almost too hard to handle, but we've always come through, stronger and more united. I promise I won't leave, no matter what. You're my home."

Yajat was deeply moved by her words. He felt a sense of clarity and certainty that he had never experienced before. Swarnima's promise resonated with him, and he knew that he needed to reciprocate her unwavering commitment.

"Swarnima," he began, his voice steady and earnest, "you've shown me what true love and partnership mean. I want you to know that I'm equally committed to our future. I've been thinking a lot about us, about what lies ahead. I want to create a life with you, one filled with love, respect, and endless adventures. I see a future where we continue to grow together, support each other. You are my heart, and I want it to be like this always!"

Yajat felt a profound sense of peace and determination. For the first time in a long while, he saw his future with absolute clarity. He envisioned a life filled with shared dreams and mutual support, a life where they could face challenges together and celebrate their victories. The ghosts of his past no longer held sway over him. Instead, he was driven by the love and commitment they shared. As they sat together, wrapped in each other's embrace, Yajat realized just how much he had changed. His notions of love, boundaries, and what it meant to truly be with someone had evolved. Swarnima had taught him to trust, to let go of his fears, and to embrace the present. In turn, he had learned to be a better partner, to listen, and to love selflessly.

That night, as they lay in bed, Yajat whispered softly, "Thank you for believing in us, Swarnima. I promise to always cherish and protect what we have."

Swarnima snuggled closer, her heart full. "And I promise to always stand by you, Yajat. Forever."

CHAPTER XVII

Closer Than Ever

The renewed closeness between Yajat and Swarnima brought a wave of intimacy and connection that neither of them had experienced before. With the past behind them, they embraced the present with open hearts and minds, weaving their lives together in beautiful and meaningful ways. On weekends, they often found themselves exploring the city, discovering new cafes, parks, and little-known cultural spots. One Sunday afternoon, they visited an art gallery that had just opened downtown. As they wandered through the exhibits, hand in hand, they marveled at the creativity and expressions around them. Swarnima, always the more adventurous one, pulled Yajat towards a section dedicated to abstract art.

"Look at this one," she said, pointing to a vibrant

painting full of swirling colors. "What do you see?"

Yajat tilted his head, studying the piece. "I see chaos and beauty intertwined," he said thoughtfully. "It's like our journey—messy at times, but incredibly beautiful."

Swarnima smiled, squeezing his hand. "Exactly. And that's why I love it. It reminds me of us."

Their days were filled with such moments of shared discovery and understanding. In the evenings, they often cooked together, turning simple meals into delightful culinary adventures. One night, as they prepared a spicy curry, Swarnima playfully smeared some sauce on Yajat's nose. He retaliated by flicking a bit of flour at her, and soon, the kitchen was a mess of laughter and love. These small, tender moments brought them closer, reinforcing the bond they had worked so hard to rebuild. Yajat, meanwhile, was gradually realizing the depth of his feelings for Swarnima. The idea of settling down with her began to take root in his mind. He often found himself daydreaming about a future where they would wake up next to each other every morning, share their lives, and build a family together. Though he hadn't mentioned it to Swarnima yet, he started taking steps towards making this dream a reality. One evening, after a particularly long day at work, Yajat came home to find Swarnima already there, engrossed in a book on the couch. He watched her for a moment, feeling a surge of affection. Quietly, he approached her and placed a gentle kiss on her forehead. She looked up and smiled, patting the space next to her.

"Join me," she said, her eyes twinkling.

As they sat together, Yajat felt a profound sense of contentment. "What are you reading?" he asked, his voice filled with curiosity.

Swarnima held up the book, revealing the title: "The Art of Happiness."

"It's about finding joy in the little things," she explained. "I thought it might be nice to explore together."

Yajat smiled, feeling grateful for her presence in his life. "I'd love that."

Their conversations often drifted to the future, and though Yajat was cautious about revealing his thoughts on settling down, he found ways to hint at his intentions. They talked about places they wanted to travel to, hobbies they wanted to pursue, and even the kind of home they envisioned living in. One Saturday, as they sat in a quaint café, sipping coffee, Swarnima mentioned her dream of starting a small garden. "I've always wanted a little patch of green," she said wistfully. "Somewhere I can grow flowers and maybe a few vegetables."

Yajat listened intently, making a mental note. "That sounds wonderful," he said. "I can see us having a garden like that. It would be perfect."

Swarnima's eyes lit up. "You really think so?"

"Absolutely," Yajat replied, his heart swelling with the thought of a shared future. "We could plant it together."

As the days passed, Yajat's resolve to make Swarnima a permanent part of his life grew stronger. He wanted to be the best partner he could be, ensuring that their love would stand the test of time. Swarnima, on her part, noticed the subtle changes in Yajat. He was more attentive, more engaged, and seemed to be planning something. Though she didn't press him, she felt a growing sense of anticipation and excitement. She loved him deeply and sensed that they were heading towards something beautiful and lasting.

One evening, after a quiet dinner at home, they sat on the balcony, gazing at the city lights. Yajat took Swarnima's hand in his, his heart racing with the enormity of his feelings. "Swarnima," he began, his voice soft and earnest, "I want you to know that you mean everything to me. These past months have shown me just how much I love you and how much I want to build a future with you."

Swarnima looked at him, her eyes filled with love and understanding. "I feel the same way, Yajat. You've brought so much joy and meaning into my life. I can't imagine it without you."

As they sat there, wrapped in each other's embrace, the future looked brighter than ever. They were ready to face whatever came their way, knowing that their love and commitment would guide them through.

As Yajat and Swarnima's relationship continued to deepen, subtle hints of differing long-term goals began to surface. These differences, though not immediately alarming, foreshadowed potential conflicts that could arise in their future together. Yajat, having experienced the turbulence of past relationships and the comfort of his current bond with Swarnima, found himself yearning for stability. He imagined a life where they settled down in a cozy home, perhaps the one with the garden Swarnima had always dreamed of. His thoughts often wandered to the idea of marriage, building a family, and creating a sanctuary where they could grow old together. These dreams brought him immense comfort and a sense of purpose. On the other hand, Swarnima, still navigating her final years of college, was filled with a desire to explore the world and discover her true passions. The thought of committing to a permanent, settled life seemed daunting to her. She cherished her independence and was excited by the possibilities that lay ahead—traveling to new places, pursuing different career opportunities, and experiencing life to its fullest. One evening, as they relaxed on their balcony, enjoying the view of the city lights, Yajat brought up a topic that had been on his mind. "Swarnima," he began, his voice gentle, "I've been thinking a lot about our future together. I know it's a bit soon, but I can't help but imagine us settling down, maybe getting married, and building a life together."

Swarnima looked at him, her eyes softening. "Yajat, that sounds beautiful, and I love the thought of being with you. But I'm still in college, and there's so much I want to experience before I can even think about settling down."

Yajat nodded, understanding but feeling a slight pang of disappointment. "I get that, Swarnima. I really do. I just... I guess I'm in a place where I crave stability. After everything I've been through, I want to know that I have a future with you, something solid to hold onto."

Swarnima took his hand in hers, her touch reassuring. "I understand, Yajat. And I want a future with you too, but I need time to figure out my path. There's so much I still want to learn and explore."

Their differing ideologies, while not immediately causing friction, began to reveal themselves in small, subtle ways. Yajat found himself making plans and decisions that aligned with his vision of a settled life, while Swarnima's choices often reflected her desire for exploration and growth. During their conversations, Yajat would sometimes discuss long-term plans, while

Swarnima would excitedly talk about internships abroad, travel plans, or new courses she wanted to take. These differences, though seemingly minor, highlighted the distinct paths they envisioned for their futures. Despite these emerging disparities, they continued to support each other, cherishing the love they shared. However, the underlying tension of their differing long-term goals lingered, a subtle yet persistent reminder that their relationship, while strong, was not without its challenges. As they navigated their present, the foreshadowing of future conflicts quietly loomed in the background, waiting to be addressed when the time was right.

CHAPTER XVIII

SHADOWS OF CHANGE

In the initial stages of their relationship, Yajat and Swarnima's bond seemed unbreakable. They spent countless hours together, sharing dreams, aspirations, and the joys of everyday life. However, as time passed, subtle shifts in their relationship dynamics began to emerge. Yajat's longing for stability and commitment clashed with Swarnima's desire to explore life and all its possibilities. While Yajat envisioned a future filled with cozy evenings and shared dreams, Swarnima found herself yearning for adventure and independence. Their conversations about the future became less frequent, as if tiptoeing around the elephant in the room. Yajat would occasionally bring up the topic of settling down, but Swarnima would quickly change the subject, her eyes lighting up with excitement as she talked about her latest travel plans or career aspirations. Despite their differing long-term goals, Yajat and Swarnima tried to avoid direct confrontations. They would often skirt around the issue, choosing instead to focus on the present moment and the happiness they found in each other's company. But beneath the surface, tension began to simmer, threatening to boil over at any moment.

One evening, as they sat together on their balcony, sipping tea and watching the sunset, Yajat couldn't help but broach the subject once again. "Swarnima," he began tentatively, "I've been thinking about our future lately. I know we've talked about it before, but I can't shake this feeling that we're not on the same page."

Swarnima's expression faltered for a moment before she quickly masked it with a smile. "Yajat, I understand where you're coming from, but I'm still young, you know? There's so much I want to see and do before I even think about settling down."

Yajat nodded, his heart sinking with each word. He had hoped that Swarnima would eventually come around to his way of thinking, but it seemed that their differences were more deeply rooted than he had realized. As the weeks passed, their interactions became more infrequent, and the distance between them grew. Yajat found himself retreating into himself, unsure of how to bridge the growing divide between them. Swarnima, too, seemed lost in her own thoughts, her once bright eyes now clouded with uncertainty. Their once vibrant relationship had begun to wither, overshadowed by the looming specter of their conflicting desires. Yajat couldn't help but wonder if their love was strong enough to weather this storm, or if they were destined to drift apart, like ships passing in the night.

As days turned into weeks, Yajat and Swarnima found themselves caught up in the whirlwind of their individual responsibilities, their once harmonious relationship beginning to show signs of strain. Despite their best efforts to maintain their connection, the frequency of their moments together grew increasingly sparse. Yajat, ever the pacifist, chose to tread carefully around their budding tensions, opting to give Swarnima the space she needed to focus on her studies and career aspirations. He understood the importance of her academic pursuits and didn't want to be a source of added pressure. Instead, he buried himself in his work, pouring his energy into his professional endeavors in an attempt to distract himself from the growing chasm between them. Meanwhile, Swarnima juggled the demands of her college life with the desire to keep Yajat happy. She cherished the moments they shared but found herself increasingly preoccupied with her studies and extracurricular commitments. As exams and projects loomed overhead, she felt torn between her academic responsibilities and the need to nurture her relationship with Yajat.

Their once-synced rhythms now seemed out of tune, their interactions becoming more infrequent and disjointed. Swarnima's absence from their shared flat during her busiest periods left Yajat feeling adrift, longing for the warmth of her presence beside him. Yet, he understood that her academic pursuits were paramount, and he respected her need to prioritize her career goals. Despite the physical distance between them, Swarnima made efforts to reassure Yajat of her commitment to their relationship. She would send him occasional messages and calls, offering words of encouragement and reminders of her affection. However, Yajat couldn't shake the nagging feeling of disconnect that lingered in the air whenever they were apart. In moments of solitude, Yajat found himself grappling with a whirlwind of emotions, questioning the future of their relationship and whether they could bridge the growing divide between them. He yearned for the closeness they once shared, longing for the days when they were inseparable. Despite the challenges they faced, Yajat held onto the belief that this was just a phase, a temporary hurdle they needed to overcome together. He remained steadfast in his faith in their love, trusting that their bond would withstand the tests of time and distance.

As Swarnima's exams drew nearer, Yajat made a conscious effort to be her pillar of support, offering words of encouragement and understanding. He reassured her that he would be waiting for her return, ready to embrace her with open arms once her academic obligations were fulfilled. In the midst of their individual struggles, Yajat and Swarnima clung to the hope that their love would endure, stronger and more resilient than ever before. And as they navigated the complexities of their separate worlds, they held onto the belief that together, they could weather any storm that came their way. During the month-long exams, Yajat and Swarnima found themselves drifting further apart, their once inseparable bond strained by the demands of Swarnima's academic commitments. Despite their best intentions, their interactions became increasingly sporadic, reduced to fleeting moments stolen between study sessions and exam preparations.

Yajat, acutely aware of the growing distance between them, struggled to reconcile his desire for closeness with Swarnima's need for space to focus on her studies. He knew that constantly calling her to the flat would be selfish, yet he couldn't shake the feeling of emptiness that gnawed at him in her absence. It was a bitter realization for Yajat, whose dreams of a future filled with love and togetherness seemed to be slipping through his fingers with each passing day. Meanwhile, Swarnima did her best to balance her academic responsibilities with her commitment to Yajat. She understood the importance of maintaining their relationship but found herself overwhelmed by the demands of her exams and projects. Despite her best efforts, she could only spare occasional moments to meet Yajat, often feeling guilty for not being able to devote more time to him.

Yajat's conflicted emotions mirrored the turmoil within him. On one hand, he was consumed by his professional life, throwing himself into his work as a means of distraction from the growing void in his personal life. Yet, on the other hand, he couldn't shake the feeling of longing for Swarnima's presence, yearning for the warmth of her embrace and the sound of her laughter filling the empty spaces of their shared flat. As the weeks passed, Yajat found himself grappling with a sense of disillusionment, his once vibrant dreams overshadowed by the stark reality of their strained relationship. He questioned whether their love was strong enough to withstand the trials they faced, whether they could bridge the growing chasm between them and find their way back to each other. Despite his doubts, Yajat refused to give up hope. He continued to give Swarnima the space she needed, understanding that her studies were her top priority. Yet, he couldn't deny the ache in his heart, the longing for a connection that seemed to slip further away with each passing day.

In the rare moments when they did manage to meet, Yajat cherished every second, drinking in the sight of Swarnima's smiling face and reveling in the warmth of her touch. Yet, even in those fleeting moments of togetherness, he couldn't shake the feeling of unease that lingered beneath the surface. As the exams drew to a close and Swarnima's schedule began to ease, Yajat held onto the hope that they could rebuild what they had lost, that they could find their way back to each other and rediscover the love that had brought them together in the first place. But deep down, he couldn't shake the fear that their bond may have been irreparably damaged, that their dreams of a future together may remain forever out of reach.

CHAPTER XIX

TUMULTUOUS TIMES

The growing differences between Yajat and Swarnima began to cast a long shadow over their relationship. What had once been a joyful and vibrant connection was now strained by their conflicting obligations and evolving priorities. Their daily interactions, once filled with warmth and affection, had morphed into something different, something colder. Yajat found himself spending more time alone in their flat, the silence a stark contrast to the laughter and shared moments that had once filled the space. His professional life was thriving, but each success felt hollow without Swarnima by his side to share it with. Their meetings had become infrequent, reduced to rushed encounters squeezed between Swarnima's academic commitments. Swarnima, too, felt the weight of their growing distance. She was consumed by her studies and the pressure to succeed, often spending long hours at the library or in study groups. Their once spontaneous and carefree conversations had become scheduled video calls, each filled with polite inquiries about each other's day but lacking the depth and intimacy they once shared. Yajat couldn't shake the feeling of unease that settled in his chest during these calls. He missed the physical presence of Swarnima, the comfort of her touch, and the simple pleasure of being together without words. He began to doubt his future plans, the ones he had dreamed of sharing with her. The thought of discussing these plans with Swarnima now seemed daunting, as he feared it would only lead to more conflict.

In the rare moments they did manage to meet, the tension between them was palpable. They both tried to hide it, putting on brave faces and pretending that everything was fine. But the truth was evident to anyone who observed them closely. Their friends noticed the changes, the way they seemed distant and preoccupied, but chose not to comment, respecting their privacy. The weight of their unspoken issues hung heavy in the air. Yajat, usually so open and communicative, found himself holding back, afraid that sharing his thoughts and fears would only drive Swarnima further away. Swarnima, too, sensed the growing divide but felt powerless to bridge it, trapped by her own responsibilities and the fear of disappointing Yajat. The once vibrant dynamic of their relationship had shifted. They were still connected by technology, by video calls and text messages, but the emotional connection that had been the bedrock of their relationship was fraying. Both of them were aware of the changes, but neither knew how to address them without causing more pain. Despite their best efforts to maintain a semblance of normalcy, the reality of their strained relationship was undeniable. The future that Yajat had once envisioned with Swarnima seemed uncertain, and the dreams they had shared felt like distant memories. As they navigated this difficult phase, both Yajat and Swarnima were left to wonder if they could find their way back to each other or if their paths were slowly diverging, leaving them to drift apart despite their best intentions.

The strain in Yajat and Swarnima's relationship was becoming increasingly evident through their frequent conflicts. Their differing priorities and increasing obligations had begun to create a rift that neither of them knew how to bridge effectively. One evening, Swarnima suggested they go out for a movie. She wanted to escape the stress of her studies and spend some quality time with Yajat, hoping to rekindle the connection they once had. "Let's catch that new film everyone's talking about," she said, her eyes bright with anticipation. "It'll be fun to get out and do something together."

Yajat, however, felt the weight of his work pressing down on him. Deadlines were looming, and the pressure to perform was mounting. "I'm sorry, Swarnima," he replied, his voice tinged with regret. "I have a lot of work to catch up on. Maybe we can go some other time?"

Disappointed, Swarnima felt a pang of frustration. "It's always work, Yajat. We never spend time together like we used to."

Yajat sighed, feeling torn between his responsibilities and his desire to make Swarnima happy. "I know, but this project is really important. I promise we'll go out soon."

On another occasion, Yajat eagerly invited Swarnima to come over to the flat for a quiet evening together. He missed the simple comfort of her presence and hoped to spend some uninterrupted time with her. "Why don't you come over tonight? We can cook dinner together and just relax," he suggested.

Swarnima hesitated, a conflicted look crossing her face. "I actually have plans with some friends tonight. We're going to this new café. You can join us if you want."

Yajat felt a twinge of irritation. It wasn't that he didn't enjoy socializing, but he had been longing for some alone time with Swarnima. "I was hoping we could have some time just for ourselves," he said, trying to keep his tone even.

Swarnima sighed. "I know, but I've already committed to this. You can come with us and we'll still be together."

The compromise didn't sit well with Yajat. He felt as though their private moments were slipping away, overshadowed by other commitments. "It's not the same, Swarnima. We hardly get any time just for us anymore."

The growing differences between them were becoming harder to ignore. Swarnima's desire to explore and engage in social activities clashed with Yajat's need for quiet, intimate moments. Each time they tried to make plans, their conflicting priorities led to disappointment and frustration. Yajat began to feel increasingly disconnected. He found it difficult to balance his demanding work schedule with Swarnima's social calendar. The times they did spend together felt strained, and their conversations often veered into arguments about their lack of quality time.

Swarnima, on the other hand, felt suffocated by the confines of the flat and Yajat's reluctance to engage in her world. She enjoyed her time with friends and exploring new places, and she wished Yajat would be more willing to join her. Each refusal from him felt like a rejection of her lifestyle, and she struggled with feelings of resentment. Despite their love for each other, the frequency of their conflicts was increasing. Small disagreements began to escalate into larger arguments, and their attempts to reconcile often left unresolved feelings lingering between them. The harmony they once shared was becoming harder to maintain, replaced by a growing sense of discontent. Their differing approaches to handling their obligations and spending time together were driving a wedge between them. The love and commitment they had for each other were still there, but the path to maintaining a harmonious relationship seemed increasingly fraught with challenges. As they navigated this turbulent period, both Yajat and Swarnima were left wondering if they could find a way to reconcile their differences or if their relationship was slowly unravelling before their eyes.

Yajat sat at his desk, his eyes staring blankly at the computer screen. The work in front of him seemed trivial compared to the turmoil brewing within. His thoughts drifted to Swarnima and the growing chasm between them. He had always envisioned a settled life, a steady routine with a partner who shared his desire for stability. Swarnima, however, had a spirit that craved freedom and exploration, and this fundamental difference was slowly but surely eroding their relationship. He remembered the early days of their relationship, filled with joy and mutual discovery. But now, every interaction seemed to carry the weight of unspoken frustrations. Yajat longed for evenings spent quietly at home, sharing intimate moments and deep conversations. Swarnima, on the other hand, thrived on spontaneous adventures and social gatherings, her zest for life often pulling her away from the domestic tranquillity Yajat cherished.

Their recent disagreements had started to wear on him. Each argument left him feeling more isolated, and he could see the same strain reflected in Swarnima's eyes. She would return late from outings, the vibrant energy that once defined her replaced by a subdued tension. Their conversations, once so fluid and engaging, now felt forced and guarded. Despite their love for each other, there was an undeniable sense that they were drifting apart. Yajat's internal struggle intensified each day. He wanted to support Swarnima's need for independence, but doing so made him feel neglected and unimportant. His desire for a settled life felt increasingly at odds with her quest for freedom. He often found himself questioning his own expectations. Was he being too rigid? Was his dream of a stable, settled life too much to ask? Yet, he couldn't shake the feeling that compromising too much would mean losing a part of himself. He feared that accommodating Swarnima's desires might lead to a life that left him unfulfilled.

Hints of an impending end loomed over their interactions. Yajat noticed the subtle changes in Swarnima's behaviour – the way she hesitated before answering his questions, the distance in her eyes when they talked about the future. She seemed to sense it too, though neither of them was ready to acknowledge it outright. They continued to hold on, each hoping that their love would be enough to bridge the widening gap. Yet, the unspoken truth was becoming harder to ignore. Yajat's heart ached at the thought of losing Swarnima, but he also feared the toll it was taking on both of them. In the quiet moments when he was alone, Yajat contemplated their future. The looming end felt almost palpable, like a storm gathering on the horizon. He knew they couldn't continue like this indefinitely. Something had to give, and he dreaded the day when they would have to confront the reality of their diverging paths. As he stared out the window, watching the city lights flicker in the distance, Yajat felt a profound sadness settle over him. He loved Swarnima deeply, but their differing desires were pulling them in opposite directions. The struggle between his need for a settled life and her yearning for freedom was reaching a breaking point, and both of them could feel the impending clash that might shatter their world.

CHAPTER XX

THE HEART'S DILEMMA

After months of restraint and avoidance, Yajat finally invited Swarnima over. The weight of their growing frustrations had become unbearable, and he knew it was time for a heart-to-heart conversation. As he tidied up the flat, he couldn't shake the nerves gnawing at him. This wasn't just another casual meeting; it was a pivotal moment that could determine the future of their relationship. Swarnima arrived, her face reflecting a mix of curiosity and apprehension. They exchanged a brief, awkward hug before settling on the couch. The silence between them was heavy, charged with the unspoken tensions of the past months.

Yajat took a deep breath, his heart pounding. "Swarnima, we need to talk," he began, his voice steady but filled with emotion. "I've been feeling this distance between us, and it's been eating me up inside. I can't keep pretending everything is okay."

Swarnima nodded, her eyes glistening with unshed tears. "I know, Yajat. I've felt it too. It's like we're both holding back, afraid to address what's really going on."

Yajat leaned forward, his hands clasped together. "I miss how we used to be, how close we were. But I also realize that we have different needs and dreams. I don't want us to keep drifting apart without trying to understand each other."

Swarnima sighed, her shoulders relaxing slightly. "I want that too, Yajat. I want to find a way to bridge this gap. We owe it to ourselves to try, don't we?"

Their eyes met, and for the first time in months, they felt a glimmer of hope. It was the beginning of a difficult conversation, but also the first step toward healing and understanding.

Yajat took a deep breath and looked at Swarnima, the gravity of the moment weighing heavily on him. "Swarnima, we've been avoiding this conversation for too long. I feel like we're drifting apart, and it's breaking me. I need to know where we stand."

Swarnima, her expression guarded, nodded slowly. "I know, Yajat. I've been feeling it too. It's like we're living parallel lives that barely intersect anymore. But what exactly do you want to talk about?"

Yajat's heart raced. "I want us to be together, Swarnima. Not just now, but in the future too. I've been thinking about us settling down, building a life together. I know we've had our differences, but I thought we could work through them."

Swarnima's eyes widened in surprise and apprehension. "Yajat, I committed to being with you, yes. But I never committed to settling down. I'm still in college. I have so much I want to do, so much I want to explore. I can't be tied down by a commitment like that right now."

Yajat felt a pang of hurt. "But I've been changing, planning, all for us. I've been trying to create a future where we can be together. Isn't that worth something?"

Swarnima shook her head, her voice trembling slightly. "It is, Yajat. It means a lot. But I can't promise you that future. I can't promise you that I'll be ready to settle down anytime soon. I need to find out who I am and what I want from life."

Yajat clenched his fists, trying to keep his frustration in check. "I understand you want to explore, but why can't we do that together? Why does it have to mean we're not committed to each other?"

Swarnima sighed, looking down at her hands. "Because it's not just about exploring places or new experiences. It's about figuring out who I am without any expectations or commitments weighing me down. I don't want to look back and regret not taking the time to understand myself fully."

Yajat's voice cracked with emotion. "So, you're saying I'm holding you back? That our relationship is a burden to you?"

Swarnima reached out, taking his hand in hers. "No, Yajat. You're not a burden. Our relationship isn't a burden. But the commitment you're asking for is something I'm not ready to give. It's not fair to either of us if I make a promise I can't keep."

Yajat pulled his hand away, running it through his hair in frustration. "I've been giving you time. I've been patient, hoping you'd come around. But it feels like the more I wait, the more distant you become."

Swarnima's eyes filled with tears. "I'm sorry, Yajat. I really am. But I can't change how I feel. I need this time for myself. I need to know who I am before I can commit to being with someone forever."

Yajat's heart sank. "So, what does that mean for us? Are you saying this is the end?"

Swarnima shook her head vehemently. "No, I'm not saying it's the end. I'm saying I need a break to figure things out. We can still be together, but I need to do this for me."

Yajat's voice grew softer, tinged with desperation. "Another break? It feels like a breakup to me, Swarnima. I don't understand this new-age definition of breaks and togetherness. For me, it means going away permanently."

Swarnima wiped away her tears. "I know it's hard to understand. It's about giving both of us space to grow individually. We've been so wrapped up in each other that we've lost sight of our own paths."

Yajat stood frozen, his mind reeling from the bombshell Swarnima had just dropped. A break? What did that even mean? In his mind, it was synonymous with the end. His worst fears, the ones that had haunted him since the beginning of their relationship, seemed to be manifesting right before his eyes. The future he had painstakingly envisioned with Swarnima was crumbling, and he felt utterly helpless. Swarnima moved around the room, her movements mechanical as she began to pack her belongings. Yajat watched in silence, his heart breaking with each item she placed in her suitcase. Every part of him screamed to stop her, to make her see reason, to beg her to stay. But he couldn't bring himself to do it. He respected her too much to undermine her need for space, no matter how much it pained him.

"Swarnima," he finally managed to say, his voice barely above a whisper. "Are you sure about this?"

She paused, looking up at him with eyes filled with a mixture of sadness and determination. "Yes, Yajat. I need this time for myself. I need to understand who I am and what I want from life."

"But what about us?" he asked, his voice cracking. "What about everything we've built together?"

She sighed, her shoulders slumping as she zipped up her suitcase. "I'm not saying it's the end, Yajat. I'm saying I need to take a step back to find clarity. It's better for both of us in the long run."

Yajat nodded, though he didn't really understand. All he could feel was an overwhelming sense of loss and confusion. "And what am I supposed to do while you're gone?"

Swarnima stepped closer, reaching out to touch his arm. "You take this time too. Reflect on what you want, on what makes you happy. We both need to grow individually before we can figure out if we still fit together."

He wanted to argue, to tell her that he had already done his growing, that he knew exactly what he wanted—her. But the words caught in his throat, tangled with his pride and fear. Instead, he simply nodded again, his eyes downcast. As Swarnima resumed packing, Yajat retreated into his thoughts. He replayed every moment of their relationship, searching for where things had gone wrong. Had he been too demanding, too focused on the future? Or had she simply outgrown him? His mind raced, trying to make sense of it all, but finding only more questions. The room felt colder without her presence, and Yajat wrapped his arms around himself, as if trying to hold on to the last bits of warmth. He watched as Swarnima finished packing, her suitcase now full. It felt like a metaphor for the emptiness he felt inside.

Swarnima looked at him one last time, her eyes glistening with unshed tears. "I'll call you, Yajat. We'll talk."

He nodded, unable to trust his voice. He watched as she walked to the door, her movements slow and hesitant. When she reached the threshold, she paused, turning back to him.

"I still care about you, Yajat. This isn't easy for me either."

He gave her a small, sad smile. "I know, Swarnima. I know."

And then she was gone. The door clicked shut behind her, leaving Yajat alone with his thoughts. The silence was deafening, and he felt like he was suffocating in the emptiness of the apartment. He sank onto the couch, burying his face in his hands. He needed to process everything, to understand what this break meant for them. He needed to come to terms with the fact that the woman he loved, the woman he had planned his future around, was no longer by his side. The hours passed in a blur as he sat there, lost in thought. Memories of their time together flooded his mind—both the good and the bad. He thought about their shared dreams, the moments of laughter, and the nights spent in each other's arms. But he also thought about their arguments, their differing ideologies, and the growing distance that had led them to this point. He knew he had to respect her wishes, but it didn't make it any easier. He felt like he was fighting a losing battle against his own emotions. He had always prided himself on being rational, on keeping his feelings in check. But now, all that control seemed to be slipping away. As night fell, Yajat finally stood up, his legs stiff from sitting for so long. He walked to the balcony, staring out at the city lights. The world outside continued to move, oblivious to the turmoil within him. He took a deep breath, trying to steady himself. He knew he had to give Swarnima the space she needed. He had to trust that if their love was strong enough, they would find their way back to each other. But for now, all he could do was wait and hope that this break wouldn't break them apart forever.

CHAPTER XXI

THE TEST OF LOVE

Yajat's days became a blur of sleepless nights and restless thoughts. The emptiness left by Swarnima's absence was overwhelming, and he struggled to fill the void. He tried to distract himself with work, pouring over projects and deadlines, but his mind always drifted back to her. The more he thought about it, the more he realized he couldn't let her go without a fight. Determined to patch things up, Yajat started reaching out to Swarnima. He sent her thoughtful messages, reminding her of the good times they had shared. He even suggested meeting up to talk things over, hoping to rekindle their connection. But Swarnima's responses were lukewarm at best. She replied sporadically, her messages polite but distant. One evening, Yajat decided to call her. He knew it was a risk, but he couldn't bear the uncertainty any longer. The phone rang several times before she picked up.

"Hello?" Swarnima's voice was soft, almost hesitant.

"Hi, Swarnima. It's Yajat," he said, trying to keep his voice steady. "I was wondering if we could meet up and talk. I miss you."

There was a pause on the other end, and Yajat held his breath.

"Yajat, I don't think that's a good idea right now," she finally said. "I need more time."

"But it's been weeks," he argued, his desperation creeping into his voice. "I can't keep going like this, not knowing where we stand."

"I understand, but I need to figure things out on my own," Swarnima replied. "It's not that I don't care about you. I just... I need space."

Her words hit him like a punch to the gut. He had hoped that time apart would bring them closer, that she would miss him as much as he missed her. But it was clear that Swarnima was not ready to come back, and he didn't know how to change that.

"Okay," Yajat said, his voice barely above a whisper. "I understand. Take all the time you need."

After hanging up, Yajat felt a crushing sense of defeat. He had tried everything he could think of, but nothing seemed to bring them closer. Swarnima was determined to stay away, and he was powerless to change her mind. Days turned into weeks, and Yajat continued to struggle. He missed her presence, her laughter, the way she made everything better. But he knew he couldn't force her to come back. All he could do was hope that, in time, she would realize that they were meant to be together. But as the days went by, that hope began to fade. Swarnima remained distant, her responses few and far between. Yajat realized that he had to accept the possibility that she might never come back, and that thought was almost too much to bear. Still, he held on to the sliver of hope that one day, things would be different. Until then, he had to find a way to move forward, no matter how painful it was.

In the quiet moments of solitude, Yajat found himself wrestling with a profound realization. The more he tried to hold onto Swarnima, the more elusive she became. Her messages were polite but distant, her voice on the phone hesitant, and her reluctance to meet spoke volumes. It was in these silent, introspective moments that Yajat began to understand something he had been too blinded by love to see: Swarnima's happiness was paramount, and her decision to seek freedom was unshakable. Every time he replayed their conversations in his mind, he could hear the undertone of her yearning for independence. Swarnima had always been a free spirit, someone who thrived on exploration and the promise of new experiences. Yajat, on the other hand, had found comfort and security in the idea of settling down, creating a life built on stability and routine. Their differing ideologies had once seemed like mere contrasts, but now they loomed like insurmountable chasms. Yajat's realization was a gradual acceptance. He recalled the way Swarnima's eyes would light up when she talked about her future plans, her travels, and the dreams she wanted to chase. These were the things that fueled her spirit, gave her life meaning, and made her who she was. To confine her to a life that didn't align with her aspirations would be to strip her of her essence. He remembered the last conversation they had, where he had tried to persuade her to come back, to give their relationship another chance. The pain in her voice as she explained her need for space, her desire to figure things out on her own, was etched into his memory. It was then he truly understood that her decision was not a reflection of his worth or their relationship but a necessary step for her own growth and happiness.

Swarnima's need to be free was not a rejection of him but an affirmation of herself. Yajat realized that true love sometimes means letting go, allowing the other person to find their own path even if it leads away from you. He had been so focused on his own desires, his own vision of a future together, that he had failed to see what Swarnima needed most: the freedom to be herself, to explore, and to grow. This realization brought a bittersweet sense of clarity. Yajat understood that his love for Swarnima meant supporting her decisions, even if they pained him. It meant respecting her choices and giving her the space she needed, even if it meant he had to endure the ache of separation. His happiness was intertwined with hers, and if her happiness lay in freedom, he had to honor that. Yajat's heart ached, but there was a new resolve within him. He would let her go, not out of resignation, but out of love. He would cherish the memories they made, the moments they shared, and hold them close as he navigated his own path. It was not the ending he had envisioned, but it was the one that honored who Swarnima was and what she needed.

Yajat took a deep breath, feeling the weight of his decision settle within him. He would carry on, knowing that he had loved deeply and truly, and that sometimes, love means setting someone free. Swarnima's happiness was more important than his own desires, and in accepting that, he found a sense of peace amidst the heartache. Yajat lay on his bed, staring at the ceiling as the reality of his situation slowly dawned on him. The room was silent, save for the occasional hum of the air conditioner, but his mind was anything but quiet. Emotions swirled within him like a storm, each thought clashing violently with the next. The impending breakup was no longer a distant possibility but a looming certainty, and he was left grappling with the weight of it all. He felt an overwhelming sense of loss, a hollow ache that gnawed at his chest. Swarnima had been the light in his life, the person who made everything seem brighter and more meaningful. The idea of waking up without her, of not hearing her laughter or seeing her smile, was unbearable. He clung to the memories of their time together, trying to hold onto the moments of joy and connection, but they slipped through his fingers like sand. Anger bubbled up within him, not directed at Swarnima, but at the cruel twist of fate that had brought them to this point. He felt angry at himself for not being enough, for not understanding her needs sooner. He was angry at the universe for bringing them together only to tear them apart. The unfairness of it all was maddening, and he wanted to lash out, to find something or someone to blame.

But beneath the anger and the sadness, there was also

a deep well of love and respect for Swarnima. He knew that her decision to seek freedom and space was not a reflection of his inadequacy but a necessity for her own growth. He admired her courage to follow her heart, even if it meant walking away from him. It was this love and respect that made it so hard to let go, that made him want to fight for what they had, even though he knew in his heart that it was futile. Yajat's thoughts drifted to the future, to the life he had envisioned with Swarnima. The dreams of a settled life, of building a home together, now seemed like distant fantasies. He felt a pang of regret for the plans they had made, for the future that would never be. But he also knew that clinging to those dreams would only prolong the pain, that he needed to find a way to move forward without her. As he lay there, Yajat realized that he was facing a crossroads. He could either wallow in his grief and let it consume him, or he could choose to honor Swarnima's decision and find a way to heal. It was a daunting prospect, but he knew that he had to find the strength within himself to let go. The impending breakup was a bitter pill to swallow, but Yajat was determined to face it with grace and dignity. He would allow himself to feel the pain, to mourn the loss, but he would also strive to find a path forward. It was not the ending he had hoped for, but he knew that it was the one that would ultimately lead them both to where they needed to be.

CHAPTER XXII

I Let You Go

Yajat sat alone in his living room, the dim light casting long shadows on the walls. It had been a month since Swarnima had left, and the silence of her absence was deafening. As he sipped his coffee, his mind drifted back to the countless moments they had shared, replaying them over and over like a favorite film. Each memory was bittersweet, a blend of joy and pain, love and loss. He remembered the early days of their relationship, when everything felt new and exciting. The late-night conversations, the shared laughter, the effortless connection—they had all felt so perfect. But as he looked back now, Yajat began to see the cracks that had always been there, hidden beneath the surface. He realized that while they were meant to be together, it was never meant to be forever.

In the beginning, he had been captivated by

Swarnima's free spirit. She had a zest for life that was infectious, a desire to explore and experience everything the world had to offer. He admired her independence and her courage to follow her dreams. But as time went on, his own insecurities and fears began to cloud his judgment. He had tried to hold onto her too tightly, projecting his own desires for stability and commitment onto her. Yajat realized now that he had been blind to the signs. He had burdened Swarnima with his need for permanence, expecting her to fulfill a role she was not ready for. She wanted to be with him, but not in the way he had envisioned. She needed the freedom to grow and explore, to find herself without the constraints of a long-term commitment. He thought about his past relationships and how different he had tried to be with Swarnima. He had wanted to avoid the mistakes he had made before, to be more understanding and less demanding. But in his efforts to change, he had swung too far in the opposite direction. He had expected too much from her, putting pressure on their relationship that neither of them could handle.

Yajat's mind wandered to his own college days, remembering the excitement and uncertainty of that time. He had been much like Swarnima, eager to experience life and reluctant to be tied down. He understood now the temptations she faced, the desire to live out her life without being burdened by commitments she wasn't ready for. He had always thought of Swarnima as his anchor, the person who brought him peace amidst the chaos of his life. But in retrospect, he realized that he had been trying to use her as a solution to his own inner turmoil. His hustle for success, his quest for stability, had all been directed towards the peace he found in her presence. He had projected his own needs onto her, without truly understanding who she was and what she wanted. The month of solitude had been a time of deep reflection for Yajat. He had replayed their conversations in his mind, seeing them now with a clarity that had eluded him before. He remembered the subtle hints she had given, the times she had expressed her desire for independence. He had ignored those signs, convincing himself that their love would be enough to bridge the gap between their differing desires.

Yajat understood now that he had been unfair to Swarnima. He had expected her to conform to his vision of the future, without considering her own dreams and aspirations. She was a free bird, not yet ready to be caged by the commitments he wanted. He realized that he had been selfish, trying to mold her into someone she was not. As the days turned into weeks, Yajat found a sense of peace in this realization. He respected Swarnima's need for freedom and understood that their paths were meant to diverge. It was a painful acceptance, but also a liberating one. He knew now that he had to let her go, to allow her the space to grow and find her own way. In the quiet of his apartment, Yajat began to rebuild his life, carrying with him the lessons he had learned. He would always cherish the time he had spent with Swarnima, but he knew that their story had reached its end. It was time for both of them to move forward, to find their own paths and embrace the future, whatever it might hold.

With a heavy heart and tear-streaked face, Yajat struggled to come to terms with the inevitable truth. His nights were filled with restless tossing, and his days felt like a blur of unending sorrow. He cried often, the pain of losing Swarnima overwhelming him. But amidst the turmoil, a realization dawned on him, sharp and sudden like a bullet: Swarnima's happiness no longer lay with him but in her freedom to explore the world on her own terms. This understanding, though painful, brought a strange clarity to Yajat. He had always thought love meant holding on, but now he saw that true love sometimes meant letting go. He had been selfish, trying to anchor Swarnima to his own dreams without considering her aspirations. It was time for him to be selfless, to put her needs above his own desires. The decision was excruciating, but Yajat knew it was the right one. He had to set her free, even if it broke him. Gathering every ounce of strength, he picked up his phone and dialed her number. His fingers trembled, and his heart raced as he listened to the ringing on the other end. This was his final act of love, the ultimate sacrifice for Swarnima's happiness. He waited, each second feeling like an eternity, ready to take the fall for the sake of her future.

The phone rang only a couple of times before Swarnima picked up. There was a silence that spoke volumes before either of them could find the words. Yajat swallowed hard, feeling the weight of the moment pressing down on him.

"Swarnima," he began, his voice steady despite the storm inside, "I just wanted to thank you for everything. You've changed me in ways I never thought possible. You showed me how to open up again, how to care deeply."

Swarnima's voice was calm, but Yajat could sense the pain beneath her composed exterior. "Yajat, what's happening isn't your fault. It's me. My mind is all over the place, and I can't seem to find clarity. You've been nothing but supportive and understanding."

Yajat nodded, though she couldn't see it. "I understand that people grow and sometimes they grow apart. It's not anyone's fault. Life just... happens. You need to find your own path, and I need to respect that."

A soft sigh came through the phone. "You mean so much to me, Yajat. But right now, I can't be what you need. I can't commit to a future when I'm still trying to figure out my present."

He felt a tear slide down his cheek, but his voice remained even. "I know. I've realized that holding on too tight only causes more pain. I never wanted to hurt you, and I'm sorry if I did. I thought I was doing the right thing by trying to build a future together, but I see now that I was ignoring what you needed."

Swarnima's breath hitched slightly. "You didn't hurt me, Yajat. You made me realize a lot about myself and what I want. I just wish I could be different right now, for you."

"I've been holding onto this rope so tightly," Yajat continued, "thinking that if I just held on, everything would work out. But I didn't realize how much it was hurting both of us. The longer I held on, the more it cut into us."

There was a long pause, the kind that fills with unspoken words and emotions too deep to articulate. "I guess this is it," Swarnima whispered, her voice barely audible.

"Yeah," Yajat replied softly. "But I want you to know that my thoughts about you, my feelings for you, they won't change. You've been an incredible part of my life. I'll always cherish our time together, and I truly wish you all the best in whatever you choose to do."

Swarnima took a deep breath, steadying herself.

"Thank you, Yajat. You've been amazing, and I hope you find happiness too. This isn't goodbye forever, it's just... goodbye for now."

Yajat felt his heart constrict, but he knew what he had to say. "Swarnima, it was always you who wanted to explore, to find yourself. I held onto you because I was afraid of losing you, but now I see that holding on is what's causing the pain."

He took a deep breath, the finality of his words settling over him. "So, with a heavy heart, I'm letting go of the rope. I'm letting you go."

Before she could respond, he gently ended the call. The silence that followed was both deafening and peaceful, a quiet acceptance of what had to be done. He sat there for a moment, phone still in his hand, feeling the weight of the final words settle in.

"I am letting you go," he whispered to the empty room, a tear slipping down his face as he finally released the grip on his heart.

CHAPTER XXIII

PEACE IN PARTING

Yajat sat in his empty room, the silence pressing in on him like a heavy weight. He had put on a tough front for Swarnima during their final call, but now, alone with his thoughts, he couldn't hold back the flood of emotions any longer. Every corner of the room seemed to echo with memories of their time together, each one a painful reminder of what he had lost. The suffocating feeling of heartbreak weighed heavily on him, and he knew he couldn't stay in this city any longer. It was Swarnima who had kept him anchored here, but now that she was gone, it felt like there was nothing left to hold him back. Without giving it a second thought, Yajat grabbed his phone and booked a cab for the airport. As he waited for the cab to arrive, he glanced at the clock on the wall. It was already 4 in the morning, the darkness outside a stark contrast to the turmoil raging within him. But he didn't care about the time or the hour; all he knew was that he needed to get away, to escape from the pain that threatened to consume him. Finally, the cab pulled up outside his building, and Yajat gathered his few belongings before stepping outside. The cool night air hit him like a slap in the face, a harsh reminder of the reality of his situation. He climbed into the backseat of the cab, the leather upholstery cold against his skin. As the cab pulled away from the curb, Yajat stared out the window at the passing cityscape. The streets were deserted at this hour, the buildings looming like silent sentinels in the darkness. He felt a pang of sadness as he watched the familiar landmarks fade into the distance, knowing that he was leaving behind more than just a city – he was leaving behind a part of himself. With a heavy heart and a determined spirit, Yajat leaned back in his seat and let the rhythm of the road lull him into a restless sleep. The journey ahead would be long and difficult, but he was ready to face it head-on, no matter where it might lead.

The cab rolled along the highway, the hum of the engine providing a steady backdrop to Yajat's turbulent thoughts. But as the minutes ticked by, his unease grew, a gnawing feeling of discomfort settling in the pit of his stomach. Suddenly, he felt a wave of nausea wash over him, his head spinning with dizziness. "Stop the cab," Yajat's voice was hoarse, barely above a whisper, but the driver heard him loud and clear. Without hesitation, the driver pulled over to the side of the road, bringing the cab to a gentle stop. Yajat stumbled out of the car, his legs feeling like lead as he collapsed onto the pavement, the cool night air offering little relief from the storm raging inside him. Tears welled up in Yajat's eyes as he sat there, his mind a whirlwind of conflicting emotions. He felt lost and alone, adrift in a sea of uncertainty. The weight of everything that had transpired between him and Swarnima bore down on him like a heavy burden, threatening to crush him beneath its weight. Suddenly, he felt a gentle hand on his shoulder, and he looked up to see the cab driver standing beside him, a look of concern etched on his face. In his hand, the driver held out Yajat's phone, its screen illuminated with an incoming call from Swarnima. Yajat's heart clenched at the sight of her name, a flood of emotions washing over him. For a moment, he hesitated, unsure of what to do. Should he answer the call and try to make things right? Or should he let it go, accepting that their relationship was over? In the end, he couldn't bring himself to face Swarnima, not when he was feeling so raw and vulnerable. With trembling hands, Yajat took the phone from the driver and switched it off, silencing the incessant ringing. He knew that he couldn't handle talking to Swarnima right now, not when his emotions were still so raw. Instead, he focused on trying to calm his racing heart, taking slow, steadying breaths as he tried to regain control of his emotions. As the minutes passed, the driver remained by Yajat's side, offering silent support in his moment of need. And although Yajat was still grappling with the pain of their breakup, he found solace in the simple act of human kindness, knowing that he wasn't alone in his time of need.

As Yajat sat on the pavement, his tears mingling with the darkness of the night, the cab driver stood beside him, a silent presence of support in his moment of anguish. Gradually, Yajat became aware of the driver's comforting hand on his shoulder, a gesture of empathy that spoke volumes without words.

"Sir, I know what you're going through," the cab driver's voice was gentle, tinged with a warmth that belied his words. "I can understand your heartbreak like a brother. It's not that I haven't been there myself."

Yajat looked up, surprised by the driver's unexpected admission. Here was a stranger, someone he had only just met, offering him solace in his time of need. It was a small comfort, but in that moment, it meant everything to Yajat.

The driver continued; his voice filled with compassion. "I feel your pain. I know it's too great for you now, but with time, everything will be normal. Why are you fixated on just one person who has gone? Move ahead. Your happiness is not about that person; it's about you, your family."

Yajat listened intently; his heart heavy with emotion. The driver's words resonated with him, striking a chord deep within his soul. It was as if the man understood his innermost struggles, offering a perspective that Yajat had been unable to see through his own pain.

"Take my example," the cab driver continued. "I cannot always keep my family happy. I try so hard, but if one day I return home without chocolates, then my child is not happy with me, my wife is angry. I try every day, but I fail. So, I can never make everyone happy."

Yajat nodded, his throat tight with unspoken emotion. Here was a man who faced his own challenges, yet he still found the strength to offer comfort to a stranger in need. It was a humbling realization for Yajat, a reminder that he was not alone in his struggles.

"Why are you trying to do so, brother?" the cab driver asked gently. "If something has happened, it must have been for a reason. Here you are, crying so far away from home, and for what? Chin up."

Yajat listened in silence, his heart heavy with the weight of the driver's words. In that moment, he realized that he had been holding onto his pain, clinging to it like a lifeline in the darkness. But now, as he sat on the pavement, surrounded by the quiet hum of the night, he felt a glimmer of hope stirring within him. As Yajat slowly rose to his feet, a sense of calm settled over him. He cast one last glance at the kind-hearted cab driver, offering him a grateful nod before turning to re-enter the waiting cab. The driver, too, returned the gesture, a silent acknowledgment of the bond they had shared in that fleeting moment of shared humanity.

As the cab pulled away from the curb, Yajat gazed out of the window, watching the city lights blur into a mesmerizing kaleidoscope of colors. In the stillness of the night, he found himself lost in thought, pondering the wisdom of the stranger's words. Amidst the chaos of his emotions, Yajat found a sense of clarity emerging from the depths of his turmoil. He understood now that in the battle between his head and his heart, it was his head that must prevail. For too long, he had clung to the hope of holding onto something that was no longer meant to be. With a heavy sigh, Yajat closed his eyes, allowing the gentle rhythm of the cab's movement to soothe his troubled mind. He knew that the road ahead would not be easy, but he was ready to face it with newfound resolve.

As the cab continued its journey into the night, Yajat felt a sense of liberation wash over him. He was letting go of the pain, the regret, and the uncertainty that had plagued him for so long. In their place, he embraced a sense of acceptance, a willingness to embrace whatever the future held in store. In the darkness of the night,

Yajat found a glimmer of hope shining bright. It was a beacon of light guiding him towards a new beginning, a chance to rediscover himself and forge a path towards happiness once more. And as the cab disappeared into the abyss of the night, Yajat knew that he was ready to face whatever lay ahead, armed with the wisdom of the stranger's words and the strength of his own resilience. For in letting go, he had found the courage to embrace the journey of self-discovery, one step at a time.

EPILOGUE

Hey Readers,

Yes, I'm talking to you. You, who has walked with me through the pages of my story. You, who has felt the highs and lows of love and loss alongside me. As I sit here, reflecting on the tumultuous journey of the past two years, I realize that sharing my tale is not just a recount of events, but a conversation—a heartfelt exchange of experiences and lessons learned.

My name is Yajat, and if there is one truth I have come to understand, it is that life is a series of unpredictable events, a blend of joy and sorrow, love and loss. None of us are wrong in our feelings, nor are we always right in our actions. We are merely human, doing our best with the circumstances we face.

Swarnima and I were two souls brought together by fate, only to be pulled apart by the very essence of who we are. Neither of us were wrong in our desires or our decisions. We were simply two people with different dreams and timelines. It took me a long time to accept that the situation, rather than either of us, was to blame for the heartbreak we endured.

Through our time together, I learned a valuable lesson: the importance of focusing on oneself. It's easy to lose sight of your own needs and aspirations when you are deeply in love. You start to intertwine your happiness with another person, believing that their presence is what completes you. But, my dear reader, happiness that depends on another is fragile and fleeting. True contentment comes from within, from pursuing your passions, from nurturing your ambitions, and from cherishing your family and friends.

The act of letting go is the most powerful thing you can do. It's not about giving up or admitting defeat; rather, it's about recognizing when a relationship is no longer serving the growth and happiness of both individuals. Letting go means valuing the other person's journey as much as your own, even if it means moving in different directions. It requires immense strength and compassion to release someone you love, understanding that their path might lead away from you.

To those of you who find yourselves in a similar situation, I urge you to focus on your own growth. Pour your energy into your work, your future endeavors, and your families. Your self-worth is not defined by your relationship status but by the person you strive to become. Be compassionate towards everyone you meet. We all carry our own burdens and histories, and kindness can be a balm to many unseen wounds.

Letting go was the hardest lesson I had to learn. I realized that I needed to let go of Swarnima because holding on to her was causing me more pain than joy. It was a love so deep that it hurt to breathe, to think, to exist without her. Yet, I had to accept that our paths were not meant to converge forever.

I still think about the "what ifs." What if we had one more chance? What if things had been different? Half of me wants to fall in love again, to feel that rush of emotions and connection. But the other half is scared, terrified of the pain that might follow. It's a risk I am not willing to take again. And so, I choose to let go, because a life of letting go, while lonely at times, can never cause the same heartache as holding on to something that is no longer there.

Closing this chapter was not something I ever wanted to do. It felt like being forced to say goodbye to a part of my soul. But in letting go, I found a new strength, a new sense of self. I realized that loving Swarnima had taught me more about myself than any other experience in my life. It taught me the depths of my capacity to care, to dream, and to endure.

So, to you, my dear reader, I say this: cherish the moments you have with those you love, but do not lose yourself in the process. Understand that people come into your life for a reason, a season, or a lifetime. And when their role in your story is over, let them go with grace and gratitude.

Life is a journey of constant learning and growth. Embrace the changes, honor your feelings, and never be afraid to move forward. The pain of letting go is temporary, but the strength it brings is eternal. Love deeply, live fully, and always, always choose compassion.

As I close this chapter, I hold on to the memories, the lessons, and the love that once was. But most importantly, I let go of the pain and the past, opening my heart to whatever the future holds.

I am letting them go.

ACKNOWLEDGEMENT

First and foremost, I would like to express my deepest gratitude to the universe for serving as my guide and illuminating my path. Without its guidance, I would not have been able to navigate the journey that has led me to this point.

I extend my heartfelt thanks to my family and friends, whose unwavering support, boundless love, and steadfast faith in me have been a constant source of strength. Your belief in my abilities has kept me motivated and inspired. A special note of thanks goes to Ram Bhaiya and Vinnu, who have been my rock, providing invaluable assistance and being there for me through thick and thin. Your encouragement and support have been crucial in helping me overcome numerous challenges.

Moreover, I am profoundly grateful to all my readers. Your continuous support and the profound love you have shown me have been incredibly motivating. Your enthusiasm and feedback have kept me going, and I am deeply thankful for each and every one of you.

To everyone mentioned and those who have supported me in ways big and small, your contributions have made a significant impact on my journey. I am truly blessed to have such a wonderful network of people in my life. Thank you from the bottom of my heart.

My world revolves around your smile.

Thank you Daddy and Ma for being there and holding my back always.

LOVE YOU ALWAYS!

ANOTHER GREAT READ

ANOTHER GREAT READ

www.ingramcontent.com/pod-product-compliance
Lightning Source LLC
LaVergne TN
LVHW091312150826
845673LV00006B/1622

* 9 7 9 8 8 9 4 4 6 2 1 2 7 *